THE COVENANT

MCCAIN CRONICLES
BOOK ONE

B.N. RUNDELL

WOLFPACK
PUBLISHING
— EST 2013 —

The Covenant
Paperback Edition
Copyright © 2023 B.N. Rundell

Wolfpack Publishing
9850 S. Maryland Parkway, Suite A-5 #323
Las Vegas, Nevada 89183

wolfpackpublishing.com

Paperback ISBN 978-1-63977-810-2
eBook ISBN 978-1-63977-811-9
LCCN 2023931887

DEDICATION

This first book of the new series brings to mind the many people that have been a part of my writing adventures, from my loving wife who has always encouraged and supported me, to the leader of Wolfpack Publishing, Mike Bray. I well remember that first inquiry I made to Wolfpack and his response, "You can write, and if you can make it into a series of at least four books, we'll publish it."

My response was, "I'll do four, fourteen, or more, as long as you publish it!" and so it began, the long road paved with over fifty books in about six years. And so, I say thanks to all that have lent a helping hand, an encouraging word, a blessed comment, a correcting nudge, and more. My family, Mike Bray and his exceptional staff, and especially to the many readers who have so faithfully been along for this amazing ride—thank you, everyone! You're the best. Without each and every one, this dream would never have been realized.

THE COVENANT

THE COVENANT

CHAPTER 1

THE COVENANT

He sensed, rather than felt, the whiff of the bullet as it passed his ear and heard the blast of the shot at the same instant. Eli dropped low on the neck of his claybank stallion, digging heels into his sides to make for cover. As the big stud lunged, the rattle of rifle fire came from the trees, and he made it to the stack of rocks that marked the edge of the timber. His dapple-grey packhorse was close on the heels of his horse and as was his custom, he did not let the dun stallion get more than two paces ahead. Eli spotted a house and barn beyond the point of trees that must have been the target or source of the rifle fire. The red dun stallion pulled up as Eli swung down, dragging his Yellowboy Winchester from the scabbard as he touched ground. A quick step and he was behind the big trunk of a sycamore, the farmhouse in sight.

The big tree with a few low branches gave him good cover, but he could easily see the farmhouse, the fields, and the trees beyond. He watched as sporadic fire came from both the trees and the house, spotting the position of each of three shooters. One, closest to the house, could have fired the shot at him, or maybe it was just a wild shot that came nigh to giving him a dirt nap. He scanned the field and house, locating each of the shooters and determined there were two shooters in the house, three in the trees. As he watched, a voice came from the trees, "Hey ol' man! Quit'cher shootin', give us the girl an' yore money, an' we'll let'chu be!"

From the house came the answer, "You stinkin' Johnny Rebs! You ain't gittin' nuthin' but what comes outta the end o' this hyar rifle!" and punctuated his answer with a blast from the window that sounded like the big boom of a Spencer.

The three shooters let loose a volley and as Eli watched, he spotted two men start from the trees, using the furrows of a fresh plowed field as they crawled between the mounds, inching their way toward the farmhouse. Eli, experienced in the ways of the renegade looters that prowled the countryside since the end of the war, recognized the way of plunderers and lowered the muzzle of his Winchester to take aim at the attackers. One of the men, obviously untrained in the way of stealthy approach, crawled on his elbows and knees, his rear end high above the furrows of dirt. Eli chuckled and aimed for the south end of the northbound crawler and dropped the hammer.

An agonizing scream told of the accuracy of the Winchester as Eli jacked another round into the .44-caliber rifle and waited for the other crawler to show himself. At the scream of his partner, the first crawler rolled to one side and lifted up to see what happened to his friend and another .44 slug found its target, ripping a furrow of its own across the shoulder of the attacker. Eli stepped behind the big trunk of the sycamore, knowing the third shooter would make a try for him, but the thunder of retreating horse hooves told of the third shooter's either lack of bravery or wisdom of retreat. Eli looked around the trunk at the two crawlers and watched as they crawled back to the trees. He could have shot again, maybe ended their suffering, but he had enough of killing from the war and chose to let them make their escape, hopefully with a well-learned lesson on looting.

He slipped his rifle into the scabbard and stepped into the saddle, reined the lineback red dun around and, followed by the packhorse, he started toward the farmhouse, but keeping in the trees until he drew near. He called out to the house, "Hello, the house! I'm friendly!" but he was welcomed by the boom of the Spencer.

The bullet clipped the leaves overhead followed by a warning, "You low-down yellow-bellied Johnny Reb! I tol' you that you ain't gettin' nuthin' that don't come outta the barrel of this hyar rifle!"

"Hold on! I'm the one that sent those outlaws runnin'! Didn't you hear my shooting from the trees back yonder?"

He heard some low talking from the windows of the farmhouse followed by "Alright! Show yerself but keep yore hands high! Try anything an' I'll blow you plumb outta yore saddle!"

Eli chuckled to himself and nudged the stallion from the trees and into the open field that lay before the house. He sat tall in the saddle, a proud man, but his countenance told of sorrow and loneliness. With many years of leading a company of cavalry into battle, his confidence and demeanor was unmistakable. While the weapons he carried—a Winchester Yellowboy repeater in the scabbard under the saddle's fender skirt, a Colt Army pistol on his hip, a new LeMat revolver in the saddlebags, and a razor-sharp Bowie knife in a sheath at the small of his back, plus his distant stare—told of purpose. Elijah McCain was on a mission prompted by a covenant he made with his wife on her deathbed, and from that he would not be swayed.

He moved the big stallion to the hitchrail, stopped with lowering both hands to rest on the saddle horn as he shifted on the seat of the saddle, looking at the door of the farmhouse. It opened a slit, the muzzle of a rifle protruding and the faint image of a man's whiskered face showing. "Go on! Git down! But keep yore hands high!"

Eli shook his head and swung his leg over the cantle of the saddle and stepped to the ground. His horse, a crossbreed between a Morgan and a Tennessee Walker with a broad blaze covering his face and three stockings, stood a good sixteen hands, but Eli stood before the animal and showed himself to be a big man standing three inches over six feet and topping the scales at just over fifteen stone, or about two hundred fifteen pounds. He wore canvas britches, a grey linen shirt, lambskin waistcoat, and a black wide-brimmed felt hat. His holstered pistol sat on his left hip, butt forward. He stood with arms folded across his chest and the old man noticed his hand was close to the pistol butt.

"Wha'chu doin' here?"

"I was just riding past when a bullet came close to partin' my hair and the rifle shots told me somebody was in trouble, so I, well, I just had to see what was goin' on and worked my way through the trees and saw three rifles firing from the trees at your house. When a couple of 'em, wearin' Confederate grey, tried crawling through your field, I thought I'd discourage 'em a little and they lit out. So…" he shrugged, letting a mischievous grin split his face as he glanced to the door to see a curly headed girl peeking out.

"Ya hungry?" asked the whiskered farmer.

"I could eat," answered Eli. "My name's Elijah McCain, and you're..." he questioned.

"I'm Ira Hess, an' that'ns Cora, muh daughter." The farmer shook his head, turning back to the door to lead the way into the house.

It was late morning, but Eli had not taken the time to eat when he rose from his blankets before starting the day. That was on the east side of Evansville, Indiana. He left Louisville, Kentucky, the ancestral home of his wife, Margaret, four days before. After fighting consumption, she implored him to "Bring my boys home," and breathed her last. They had spent almost a year on her family's horse farm where her family raised some of the best Morgan and crossbreds in the country. His claybank lineback red dun had been one of their prize stallions and Eli chose him for his anticipated long journey to find the boys, twins, that were his stepsons. Their mother was married to his best friend, a fellow graduate of West Point, who had been killed while serving at Jefferson Barracks in St. Louis, before the boys were born. Eli was also stationed there and before his friend, Lieutenant Ferdinand Paine, died, his friend had a premonition about the impending danger and bid Eli to take care of his wife. Before Eli left for his new post at Fort Laramie, Nebraska Territory, they were married. She returned to Louisville for the birth of her children, and he left for his new post. Twin boys, Jubal, and Joshua, who at sixteen, joined the Union to fight in the war, but after their first skirmish, deserted and went west. That was the covenant he made with his wife, to bring the boys home.

The smell of frying bacon brought his thoughts back

to the present and he dropped his arms to follow Ira into the home. It was a pleasant home, the woman's touch was evident, but the only family present were the whiskery faced old man and the young girl. Eli looked around, saw a few tintypes framed and sitting on a buffet with a crocheted doily. It was a homey place, but it was also evident that those in the tintypes were missing.

Ira motioned him to be seated at the table and Ira seated himself opposite. Cora served them with plates already filled with eggs, bacon, potatoes, and biscuits. Eli smiled and said, "My, this is a meal fit for a king! Thank you."

"You're welcome, sir. Enjoy," replied a smiling Cora, wiping her hands on her apron before seating herself. Eli started to stand as she sat down but was motioned down by Ira. As she was seated, Ira grasped her hand in his and nodded to Eli, "Let us give thanks," and began with a prayer of thanksgiving for the food and their new friend. After his "Amen," Eli echoed with the same and looked up to see both the farmer and the girl smiling.

"It's not often we have comp'ny," she began, "and to have a believer is a blessing."

Eli smiled and said, "The Lord has been with me for many years now and I have learned to depend on Him every day."

"Were you in the war?" asked Ira, digging into his food with just a glance to their visitor.

"I was," replied Eli, taking a long sip of hot coffee. "You?"

"No, but I lost muh boy early on, it plumb kilt muh woman to lose her boy," he shook his head at the memory, glancing to the girl who had dropped her eyes and busied herself with her food.

"I have a couple boys that were in the war, somewhere out west now," mused Eli.

"I didn't think you were old enough to have boys that were in the war," answered Cora.

"They'd be going on nineteen now," explained Eli, making short work of the plate of food before him. He looked at Cora, "Mighty fine cooking, miss."

She dropped her eyes, smiled, and said, "Thank you, sir."

Eli looked at Ira, "The shooters, did you know them?"

"No, shore din't. But I seen them bits of uniforms they was wearin' and had heard 'bout some that was deserters and such that was stealin' an' killin' anybody what they could, so, I reckoned that'd be what they was. Some o' th' neighbors said he thought some of 'em were workin' with the money folks, them what some're callin' carpetbaggers, that're goin' to the south and buyin' properties an' such. Some of 'em think they can do the same hereabouts." Ira shook his head and mumbled, "Wouldn't s'prise me none to know the banker in town's one of 'em."

Eli frowned, looking at the man, "What makes you say that?"

"Oh, I had to take out a loan so I could put in muh crops last year'n this'n. He, the banker, was mighty short with me this time, threatened to take muh farm if'n I was even a day late on the repay'n'. Said he could put the money to better use goin' south an' buyin' farms."

"This bank, is it the one in Independence?" asked Eli.

"Ummhmm, Boatmen's bank."

Eli pushed back from the table, reached for his coffee, and held it for Cora to refill it. He took a sip and looked over the cup at Ira, "You build this farm, Ira?"

"Did. Cleared the fields, put in the crops, built this

house," he motioned around, looking at his home with pride, "raised a family."

"You've done well. It would be a shame to lose it to someone like that." He paused, sipped his coffee, and looked at the man with a glance to the girl and back. "Maybe I could help with that," he said, and let a slow grin split his face.

pastor."

CHAPTER 2

INDEPENDENCE

Ira and his daughter, Cora, rode side by side in the buckboard. Eli rode alongside on his flashy red dun stallion as the dapple-grey packhorse trotted behind. As they neared the town, a new church building stood proudly just off the main road and a man was busy planting flowers in a planter beneath the sign. Ira drew his buckboard to a stop, leaned forward, and spoke to the man busy with the plants, "Pastor, looks like yore doin' a mighty fine job with those plants. Never thought I'd see the pastor gettin' his hands dirty!" chuckled Ira.

The pastor stood, brushing the dirt off the knees of his trousers, and dropping the small trowel he used for planting. He grinned at Ira and Cora, "And how are the Hess' this fine day?"

"Oh, we're fine, pastor." He motioned to Eli and said, "I'd like you to meet a new friend of ours, pastor. This hyar is Elijah McCain, from outta Louisville an' bound fer St. Louis."

Eli stepped down and pushed the head of his stallion

around and reached out his hand, "Pleased to meet you, pastor."

"I'm Lucas Posey, Mr. McCain, and it's pleased I am to make your acquaintance. Are you leaving right away, or will you be here for the Lord's Day?"

"Oh, we're just doin' a little business with the banker and then I'm on my way."

The pastor was wide-eyed as he lifted his eyebrows to look to Ira in a question. Ira responded with, "It's that new banker, Baumann. He's threatenin' to take my farm if'n I'm even a day late, an' what with the weather an' such, he's got me a little concerned. So, Eli here said he might be able to help with that."

The pastor looked from Ira to Eli and back to Ira, "You're not the first one that has shared that information with me. Your neighbors, the McCalls and the Evans, have been told the same thing. It seems this new banker is more concerned about the bank or himself than he is about the people of our community."

"Have you heard of any connection between the banker and the rebels that have been terrorizing the farmers?" asked Eli, his frown showing his concern.

The pastor frowned, put his hand to his chin and resting his elbow on his arm across his chest, he looked up at the two men, "It's nothing certain, but there have been those that talk and wonder about it. It seems both the McCalls and Evans were hit by them, fortunately neither lost much, but what they did lose could make it more difficult for them to meet their loan."

Eli looked at Ira and with a slight nod, he mounted up and leaned on his pommel, "Pastor, we'd appreciate if you keep our little talk under your hat, and hopefully we can put a stop to this." With a nod from Ira, they pulled away, bound for the bank in Independence. Although considered part of Evansville, and originally called Lamasco City, its business area was growing due to the industrial businesses, factories, furniture makers, and coal mines, that were the lifeblood of the town. The many farms to the west of the town occupied the choice property that many of the townspeople thought necessary for the city's growth, although the farms provided most of the food for the entire area.

Ira pulled up at the livery that sat high on the shore of the Ohio River, overlooking the wide bend of the river where many of the paddle wheel riverboats were moored. He looked at Eli, "Might as well put yore horses in a stall. We might be a while; you know them bankers."

"How far is the bank?" asked Eli, stepping down.

"Tain't fer. Just a couple these blocks. It be o'er on the corner of Wabash and Fourth."

"And your lawyer friend?" asked Eli.

"Right acrost the street from the bank."

———

WHEN THEY STEPPED into the bank, the two tellers looked up but paid little attention as they were busy with other customers at their windows, but a young man in a linen shirt, a string tie, and garters on his arms, looked at the three with a frown. He stood, looking over the three as if they were in some way less than acceptable as customers of the bank. He gave a frosty, "May I help you?" to them as he cocked one eyebrow up and glared with the other eye.

Ira stepped closer, "Yup, need to see Baumann."

"That's *Mr.* Baumann! And who shall I say is asking?"

Cora stepped closer, "Oh, don't give us that, Wilbur. You know good and well who we are," and waved her hand as if she was dusting off the railing, "now go ahead and tell him!"

The young man stuttered as his face turned red and he turned on his heel and walked to the windowed door with *Mr. Baumann, President* written on the glass. He rapped on the door and opened it a little way, stuck his head in and could be heard announcing the customers. With a nod, he turned and motioned them to come through the banister railing and to the door. He opened the door wide and stepped back, letting them pass.

As they stepped into the office, Eli saw the door behind the desk slowly close as the man behind the desk stood and extended his hand to shake, painting a smile on his face that was as phony as the man's hairpiece that did little to hide his bald pate. Both Ira and Eli shook hands with the man as Ira introduced Eli as a close friend and business associate, as Eli had suggested. Baumann frowned as he looked at Eli, and slowly seated himself as the others were seated. "Business associate?" he asked, looking from Ira to Eli.

"That's right. I've looked over several properties in the area and will be investing in some, beginning with the Hess farm," explained Eli, looking at the bank president with his usual confident bearing.

"Oh, I see. And Ira, what is your business with us today?" asked Baumann, putting his elbows on his desk, and putting his fingers tip to tip before him.

Ira plopped a small leather drawstring pouch on the banker's desk, "I wanna pay off my loan!"

The banker frowned, "But Ira, that's not due till harvest," and reached for the bag. He pulled it open and dumped out ten double eagle gold pieces on his desk, making his eyes flare wide. "My!" He stacked the coins, counting them as he did and nodded to his assistant,

Wilbur, obviously sending him for the paperwork on the loan.

When Wilbur lay the papers on the banker's desk, Eli reached for them but was stopped by the banker. "Excuse me! These are only for Mr. Hess or myself," and drew them closer. Eli looked to Ira, and with a nod from the man, reached for the papers again. It was evident that the banker did not like this stranger looking at the paperwork, but with Ira's permission, he could not refuse.

Eli quickly flipped through the papers, noting the rates and terms, and glanced up at the banker, scowling and shaking his head. He looked to Ira, "Ira, since you said you could not read, did anyone, other than the banker here, explain these terms to you?"

"Uh, no, no one. It was just me'n him."

"And he gave you one hundred and fifty dollars?"

"Yup."

"And how much did he say you would have to pay him come harvest?"

"Two hundred."

Eli looked at the banker, who dropped his eyes, yet his anger was showing as his nostrils flared and he fingered the edge of his desk. Eli asked, "Are you familiar with the Federal Banking Acts of 1863 and 1864?"

"Yes, yes, of course, but...but..."

Eli shook his head, reached for the stack of coins, and took two coins from the nearest stack, handing them to Ira. Eli explained to Ira, "What he was doing is against the law. He was charging you what would be about sixty-seven percent interest. That is exorbitant and against the law for federally chartered banks. What he was doing, since he could not show that on the books, was putting that extra in his own pocket. That is what they call thievery!" he declared, scowling at the banker.

"But, you don't understand! Loaning money on farms in this time is very high risk and because of that risk, we require a greater return. That *is* legal!" he insisted.

Eli stood, leaned on the front of the banker's desk, "Mr. Baumann, *that* is not legal. I have done business with banks for many years, and I could buy and sell this bank and you with it! Now, I suggest you reexamine your books and make things right with your other customers and do it right quick. Otherwise, you're going to have a run on this bank and you both will be out of business! Do you understand?"

The banker fumed, leaning back in his chair, and said with a raised voice, "I don't know who you think you are to come into *my* bank and make such outlandish demands."

Eli smiled, replied softly, "Then I suggest you talk to my good friend, Hugh McCulloch."

Baumann's face dropped, his eyes flared, and he leaned forward, looking at Eli with obvious fear in his eyes, "Your *friend?*"

"Yes, Hugh is a longtime family friend. My family has had many occasions to entertain Hugh and his lovely wife, Susan, at our home in Maryland. Both our families were longtime successful shipbuilders, the two largest, actually." He paused as he smiled at the banker, knowing the man had recognized the name of the Comptroller of Currency, the national overseer of all federal banking activities. "Now, if you will have your man finalize those papers, marking them paid in full and signing off on them, we'll be leaving. Oh, and if your friends," he nodded toward the back of the bank and the door that had closed, "try to do anything unseemly, we'll be back here to 'talk it over' with you."

"My friends?" frowned the man.

"Yes, those men that left your office just as we came in, those three men that appear to be your, shall we say, enforcers?"

"I have no idea what you are talking about, sir," snarled the banker, motioning to his assistant to finish the paperwork.

With the completed paperwork in hand, Eli, Ira, and Cora walked across the street to the law office of Jonathan Fischer. As they were seated before the lawyer's desk, Eli explained, "Mr. Fischer, Ira and some of the other farmers have had a little difficulty with the business practices of the banker, Baumann. We just left his office, and I would like to have you draw up some papers that would make me, or the company known as McCain Investments, a part owner of his farm. This will serve as a pattern for future similar papers. Now, this is not to hinder the operation or true ownership of the property but will serve only to prevent the bank or any other lender from foreclosing and getting a clear title. Anytime a foreclosure would be pending, my company would have to be notified, and my attorneys back east will enter the picture to prevent such foreclosure. But if anyone willingly wants to sell, then we will gladly sign off for that to happen."

The lawyer looked from Eli to Ira, "Are you sure, Ira?"

"Yes, I am sure. Eli has he'ped me already and tol' the banker where he was wrong. I want to help muh neighbors the same way."

"I will give you the name and address of my company and our attorneys. Also," and he handed the lawyer five twenty-dollar greenbacks, "that should cover your fees for this and future transactions. If you need more, just write our company and you will be promptly paid."

As THEY LEFT the edge of town, Eli reined up and handed a pouch of coins and greenbacks to Ira. "Use that to help your friends in the same way we just did, paperwork and all, and that should keep the banker from trying to steal the farms from your friends."

"Eli, I shore don' know how to thank you, nosirree, I don't."

Eli looked at Cora, "Young lady, since you know how to read, you will need to help your father, maybe even teach him to read, but at least help him and your neighbors like you saw today."

"I will, and mighty proud I am to do it too, sir."

"I'll drop a letter from time to time, just to see how you're doing."

"We'll keep you in our prayers," responded Cora, smiling at the big man.

Eli tipped his hat, turned off the road and took to a trail that would take him through the thick woods toward the west. He had a long way to go, but he turned in his saddle to wave goodbye to his new friends. They returned the wave, and he could hear Cora shouting, "Goodbye, Eli!"

He grinned and nudged the big stallion into the trees, turning his thoughts to his own goal and purpose. He was hopeful to find his sons soon and fulfill his promise to his wife. He glanced heavenward, "Thank you, Lord, for letting me help your people. Now, please guide me to my sons."

CHAPTER 3

MT. VERNON

E li sat before his little cookfire, waiting on his morning coffee, as he slipped the folded paper and wrapped tintype from the saddlebags. He looked around his campsite, deep in the hardwood forest and off the road, he chuckled to himself knowing this had been the traditional territory of the Shawnee, Chickasaw, and other smaller tribes, but most had been taken by the Indian Removal Act of 1830 and had been on reservations in the area known as Indian Territory. There was no danger of Indian attack now, but there were many displaced men from the war that were rampaging the land, seeking revenge and restitution for what they lost in the war. He turned his attention back to the missive as he unfolded the paper and reread the words of his sons.

Dear Mom,

We are well and in St. Louis. By the time you receive this, we will be long gone. Jubal thinks we should go to work for the railroad as they are recruiting workers now, but I favor going with a wagon train. We talked with a wagonmaster that was looking for men to help with the train, hunting, scouting, and more. Although that does not pay as well, the work would be more rewarding, and we would see more of the West. There are also steamships looking for workers to go upstream on the Missouri to the distant trading forts. Once we decide, I shall write another letter to let you know and where you might send a letter.

We have met others that left the army, both north and south, and most are like us, just tired of killing and being shot at, but it was more than that, it was the not knowing what would happen or what our life might be if we even survived. I never told you before, but Jubal and I argued many times about joining up. He wanted to go with the South and I wanted only the blue of the Union. As you know, we both went with the Union, but Jubal couldn't find it in himself to pull the trigger on the boys in grey.

I know father will be angry when he finds out we deserted, but I would rather have an angry and disappointed father, than a weeping mother. Keep us in your prayers, Mother, for there are many dangers and temptations we face constantly. Jubal's temper had often been a challenge for us, but we will stay together and hopefully be safe.

Always remembering you and home, we are grateful for all your love and more.

Your sons,

Joshua and Jubal

Eli shook his head as he carefully folded the letter and replaced it in the envelope. He unwrapped the tintype and looked at the picture of the boys and their mother. She was seated and the boys stood behind her, each with a hand on a shoulder of their mother, the other holding their uniform hats called the Hardee Hat. The boys had never been known to wear a stoic or somber expression and were showing broad smiles for the picture.

Good-looking young men, they were tall, close to six feet, with broad shoulders, tapered hips, and dark curly hair. As Eli looked at the picture, he just could not think of them as cowards or deserters. Although he had not been home during most of their childhood, being stationed at Fort Laramie in Nebraska Territory during most of that time, their mother had raised them with a firm hand and a warm heart. They had a good education, had spent the year before enlisting at the university in Louisville and Joshua had considered studying medicine, but those plans were put aside when they chose the military.

He rewrapped the tintype and replaced both letter and picture back in his saddlebags. He poured himself some coffee and looked at the sky, now greying to early morning and appearing to be clear of any cloud cover. He grinned a little, sipped his coffee, and looked about his little camp. He breathed deep, lifting his shoulders, and stood. Finishing off his coffee, he tossed out the dregs, sat the pot and cup on a rock to cool, and went to the horses to prepare for the day.

With the horses saddled and rigged, Eli covered the ashes of the fire with dirt, and stepped to the dun to climb aboard. He had no sooner seated himself in the Western-style California saddle than he heard the sound of a wagon. The creak of wood, rattle of trace chains, and the moan of wheels on dry axles, turned his attention toward the road. He sat still, looking through the trees, as a wagon moved westward on the roadway. From what he could see, it was a Conestoga wagon driven by a young man, an older woman seated beside him, and two girls looking out the back of the wagon. Pulled by a four-horse hitch of farm horses, the wagon moved along well, stirring the little creatures of the woods to scatter and scold them as they passed.

He gave them a little while to move on their way before he pushed through the trees to take to the road. The previous two days had been long days of travel from Evansville and the next town, just a short ways ahead, would be Mount Vernon. He preferred to be on the move, but also knew the times of solitude gave too much time for thought. His years spent as a cavalry officer had been full of constant activity, from fighting Natives in the West, to fighting Confederates in the East and South. Whenever he could finagle a leave, he would travel back to see his family, but those times were few and usually too short. He breathed heavily as he thought about the many times and places he had served, the faces of the past usually coming back to haunt him.

The bridge across the little creek pointed the way to the new village of Mt. Vernon. Once across Casey Creek, the road kept to the southwest edge of the community, but the main road to the town branched off where the Mt. Vernon Inn sat. Several horses were standing hipshot at the hitchrail, the morning's breakfast undoubtedly the main attraction for the inn. With his panniers and parfleche loaded with supplies, Eli saw no reason to stop and pushed on past the edge of town. A sign at a road junction told of the Goshen Road, that Eli knew would take him to Illinoistown, just across the Mississippi from St. Louis. He glanced to the sky, thinking about his journey, and guessing it would be about three days travel to St. Louis, where his search for his sons would begin in earnest.

It was irregular country, the terrain of thickly forested hills, swales, and swamps, caused the roadway to meander through the countryside. Eli had just looked up at the sun, knowing it was nearing midday, when a shot sounded somewhere ahead. He frowned and slipped his rifle from the scabbard to lay it across his pommel and continued on his way. With the twists of the road and the thick woods, he could not see too far ahead, but shouted voices that bore the tone of anger, stopped him. He listened, heard another shot, and knew whatever was happening was not too far ahead. He nudged the big stallion and the packhorse into the trees, stepped down, and tied them off.

There had been many times in his past when he had to use all his skills at stealth to approach some hidden danger, whether angry Natives or frustrated rebels, and with that same furtiveness, he moved silently through the thick woods. Within moments, the situation showed itself where the wagon that had passed his camp in the early hours, now stood still. Two mounted men sat their horses before the wagon, pistols pointed toward the two on the seat, while two more approached the back of the wagon. Eli remembered the young girls that had shown themselves earlier, and knew they were in danger of discovery and the probability of being taken by the outlaws.

Eli moved through the trees to a point where he was slightly behind the mounted men and stepped out. He had not been seen and jacked a round into the chamber of his rifle, the rattle of the lever action sounding loud in the quiet forest. "Don't move!" he demanded, keeping his voice low. The two mounted men had started to turn, but his voice stopped them. "Drop those pistols, now!"

One of the men started to turn, but Eli repeated, "Now!" and the man moved his hand with the pistol out to the side and dropped it to the ground. The second man did likewise. Eli stepped a little closer, "Call the others back!" he ordered.

Again, the first man started to turn, but the "Don't do it!" from Eli stayed his action. "Now call them back!"

One of the men at the back of the wagon stepped out from behind it and brought his pistol up, but Eli saw the movement, and swung his rifle and fired. The bullet blossomed red at the man's chest as he dropped his pistol and grabbed at his wound, eyes flaring with fear as his knees weakened and he crumpled to the ground. Eli jacked another round just as the first mounted man grabbed for his rifle in the boot at the side of his pommel, but Eli's bullet tore through the man's shoulder, dropping him to the neck of his mount. The woman on the seat of the wagon clasped both hands to her mouth as the young man put his arm around her shoulders, drawing her close. He looked at Eli with wide eyes but moved no further.

Eli swung the rifle toward the second mounted man as he jacked another round, and called out, "You in the back, come around here with your hands empty and raised high!"

The second mounted man reached for his partner that was struggling to breathe and keep his seat on his saddle. "You alright, Angus?" he asked, trying to help him upright.

Movement at the back of the wagon caught Eli's attention as the last man came from the side, his arm around the neck of one of the young girls. He cackled as he looked at Eli, "Now what'chu gonna do, mister? You better be puttin' down yore rifle, or I'll kill this'n!"

"Come round'chere! Angus's been hit!" called the mounted man.

Eli stepped a little closer to the wagon, glaring at the

man with the girl, but not lowering his rifle. The brigand snarled again, "I tol'ju, put it down or I'm gonna kill 'er!"

Eli paused, looked at the man, and spoke softly, "Alright, alright, I'll put it down." He could see the pistol in the man's hand was a single-action Remington that had to be cocked before it could be fired, and the hammer rested against the receiver. Eli said, "Take it easy, I'm putting it down," and began to bend at the knees and lower the rifle. As he did, his jacket hung open, but the outlaw did not see what Eli was doing. By holding the rifle in his left hand by the forward stock, he appeared to be setting it down on the butt plate, a normal action that most men did to lower a rifle. But with his body slightly turned, Eli reached inside his jacket and wrapped his fingers around the butt of his Colt, withdrawing it from the holster, his thumb on the hammer. He released the rifle and it fell forward to the ground, the outlaw watching.

When Eli started to stand, he brought the pistol out, cocking it and aiming it in one smooth motion. He dropped the hammer as he brought it level and the big pistol boomed. The slug took the captor in the face, driving him back as he dropped his pistol and grabbed at his face with both hands. The girl fell to the side, and Eli fired the second time, the bullet striking the man under the chin and blowing out the top of his head.

Eli spun on his heel, bringing the pistol to bear on the two mounted men, but their surprise had been complete and both men had not moved. The wounded man slowly slid to the ground, unconscious, and the last of the outlaws glared at Eli, wide eyes full of fear. He lifted his hands high, "I ain't doin' nuthin'!" he shouted.

"Get down from there and load up your friends and get away from here before I send you to join them permanently!" ordered Eli. He watched as the man swung down, struggled to lift the downed man back to his horse, but the man was still unconscious, so he draped him over the saddle and led the other horses to the back of the wagon. He struggled to load the other two bodies to their horses and with a glance back to Eli, he mounted up and started down the road, leading the three loaded horses.

Eli looked at the woman who sat on the seat of the wagon, shaking her head, until the two girls came around the front chattering and asking questions. "Oh, Momma! Are you alright? Those men were...were...they were going to take us!"

The second girl could not say more, but looked at Eli and quietly said, "I don't know who you are, but you saved us. Thank you."

"I'm Elijah McCain, and you're welcome."

The girl said, "I'm Nora Hamilton, and that's," nodding to the girl who stood by the wagon wheel, reaching up to hold her mother's hand, "Millie. My mother is Harriet, and my brother is Benjamin."

"Pleased to meet you, folks. Sorry for the turmoil but those men had, well, nothing good in mind, I assure you."

CHAPTER 4

SHILOH

"Sir, if you're going our way, would you mind traveling along with us?" pleaded Harriet Hamilton, still holding tight to her son, Benjamin.

Eli let a slow smile split his face as he nodded, "I am going your way, and I would not mind traveling with you, for a way. But first, I must fetch my horses." He tipped his hat to the woman, nodded to the girls, and turned back to work his way through the trees.

As he came back alongside the wagon, Eli nodded and grinned as the girls craned around from behind their mother to look at their rescuer and the fine horses. Nora said, "My, that is a beautiful horse!" looking wide-eyed at the claybank stallion.

"Thank you, but don't say that too loud, he might let it go to his head and then I'd have my hands full trying to convince him I'm still in charge!" chuckled Eli, reaching down to stroke the big horse's neck. "And, my little grey mustang," nodding to the packhorse, "might feel a little slighted!"

Both girls looked from the horses to Eli and back.

Nora was the first to giggle, prompting the same from her sister. "You're kidding!" she laughed, smiling broadly.

Benjamin had started the team moving with a slap of the reins and did his best to look stern and in control. Eli guessed him to be all of fourteen or fifteen, but well setup for his age. His shoulders were filling out and stretching the homespun shirt tight across his chest. His canvas trousers showed wear with patches on the knees, and his hobnail boots were scuffed but sturdy. "You're doing a fine job handling those horses there, Benjamin. Did you use them on the farm?"

"Yessir. I used them in a double hookup or four abreast to plow the fields," answered Benjamin, sitting a little straighter and drawing his shoulders back, pride showing in his eyes.

Eli looked at Mrs. Hamilton, "Ma'am, if you don't mind my asking, it seems like a risky thing to be traveling in this country without your man nearby."

Harriet frowned, "Is there a question in that, Mr. McCain?"

Eli chuckled, dropping his eyes, "Yes'm. Reckon there is."

"Well," she began, her hands in her lap, "since you came to our aid and seem to be a man that can be trusted, my husband, Cyrus, went west when he first came home from the war. That was almost three years ago. We are traveling alone because he sent for us to join him."

"I see. And how far west are you going?" he paused, adding, "I only ask to determine how long we may be traveling together."

"Well, I guess that would also depend on how far you are traveling, Mr. McCain." The woman dropped her head to look at Eli from under her lowered brow, one eyebrow lifted as in a question.

"Good point, ma'am. But to answer that, I don't rightly know how far I'll be going. You see, I'm on a quest to find my two sons, twins, who left home in '65 and I don't rightly know where they might be found."

Harriet frowned, shaking her head slightly and crossing her arms at her waist, "I'm sorry to hear that, Mr. McCain. And their mother?"

Eli paused, dropped his eyes and looking down the road, answered softly, "She's in Heaven, ma'am."

Harriet frowned the more, shaking her head, but saying nothing. Sorrow was a way of life with many families—so many lost loved ones and homes in the war and the road was heavy with tears and castoffs as people lightened their loads and their hearts, moving west to find a new life. "Were you in the war, Mr. McCain?"

"Yes, ma'am. I was a career soldier, West Point, and all that, but no more. And it would be easier if you would just call me Eli."

"Thank you, and I answer best to Harriet."

"Well, Harriet," began Eli, glancing to the sky, "it's about time to have some coffee and maybe something to eat as well as give the animals a bit of a rest. That," nodding to a break in the trees showing a small meadow with what appeared to be a bit of a creek, "looks like a likely place to stop and take care of the stock. I'd be pleased to share my coffee with you, and I also have a bag of some venison jerky, if you'd care for some."

"Thank you, Eli," answered Harriet, putting her hand on Benjamin's arm, and motioning to the flat beside the road. It appeared to be an oft-used camp and offered a fire ring and some logs for seats. Eli helped Benjamin with the horses, rubbing down his own and helping

Benjamin tend to the teams. After the horses were watered, they picketed them on some grass, although much of the nearby grass had already been grazed on by previous travelers. As they walked back to the camp, Eli started, "So, you've been the man of the house for a couple years now. I noticed the barrel of a shotgun beside the seat, have you used that much?"

"Just for hunting, you know, birds, rabbits, squirrels. But Ma's got her pistol she keeps handy. She was 'bout to use it when you came along," he chuckled. "And she's deadly with that hand cannon, too!" he declared.

"What is it?"

"It's a Colt Dragoon, .45 caliber. And she keeps an extry cylinder loaded, too. Whenever you see her hands on her lap, the pistol is right under that apron!" he grinned.

"Smart woman," replied Eli, nodding. "But you'll find that most highwaymen will be more afraid of the shotgun in your hands than her pistol."

Benjamin frowned, "You think so?"

"That's right. Two reasons, you're almost a man and the shotgun will make up the difference. Everyone knows it's mighty hard to miss with buckshot and that can tear a man up even if you come close. Some of the cavalrymen carried them, short ones, and used them one-handed in the war. They were deadly!"

"Were you in the cavalry, Eli?"

"I was," but the shortness of his answer offered no explanation and Benjamin fell silent.

———

THE LITTLE FIRE was already going, the coffeepot dancing, and a pan of bacon sizzling when Eli and

Benjamin walked into the little camp. Eli smiled, "Well, I take it my jerky did not appeal?"

Harriet smiled, "Oh, I just thought we would make use of the leftover biscuits and a little bacon. It's not much, but a warm meal always sits better when we have a long way to go."

"It does indeed," replied Eli, seating himself on one of the logs. Nora brought him a cup and poured him some coffee as the others watched.

Harriet asked, "Would you ask the Lord's blessing on our meal, Eli?"

Eli looked up, wide-eyed. He was not one for praying aloud or among others, but he was cornered, and he doffed his hat, and with a nod to the others, he stumbled through a brief prayer of thanksgiving. When he said, "Amen," the others echoed, and he breathed easier as Harriet handed Millie a plate with a couple biscuits and meat and nodded toward Eli for her to deliver the plate. The young girl, who Eli guessed to be about ten and her sister, Nora, to be about twelve, smiled and delivered the plate with a nod.

Eli looked up at Harriet, "I answered your question about my traveling west, but somehow you seemed to evade that question. Are you ready to answer now?" he asked, grinning as he sipped his coffee.

"We are going to Virginia City, Montana Territory. My husband has been there a little more than a year and has what he says is a profitable gold claim. He is building us a home in the new settlement of Helena, and we are anxious to be reunited."

"I would imagine you are, but that is a mighty far piece to travel. Have you already made plans as to just how you're going?"

"What do you mean?"

"I mean by wagon," nodding to their wagon, "or steamboat, or train, or wagon train, or...?" he shrugged, cocking his head to the side, awaiting her answer.

"Well, I guess that depends on what might be available and..." she began, her eyes showing a question and a touch of fear. "Cyrus took a horse out to Colorado Territory because of the gold strike there, but his letters told of him going north by horse and by wagon with some other prospectors. He never traveled by any other way and I s'pose he just didn't think of that. He did send us some money..." she shrugged.

Eli could tell she was concerned but determined, and interjected, "Well, that's not to worry about now. First thing is to get to St. Louis. Then we can look into all the possibilities and decide. How's that sound?"

Harriet breathed what he thought was a touch of relief and nodded to him. "Would you care for some more biscuits?"

"No, ma'am. That was plenty. If I eat too much at midday, I'll fall asleep and end up in the middle of the road watching my horses trotting away!" he chuckled. "Maybe if we can put a few miles behind us, we can make Shiloh by mornin'."

———

THE LITTLE SETTLEMENT of Shiloh was bathed in the golds and oranges of the setting sun as the lone wagon and outrider rode in keeping to the well-traveled road that split the town, the business section on one side, homes on the other. But a large log structure seemed to cast a shadow over the town as the sun settled behind it, the cross on the belltower haloed by the setting sun. As they neared, Eli read, *Shiloh Methodist-Episcopal Church*,

Founder Rev. William McKendree, 1807. They pushed on through the town, watched by a few folks sitting in rocking chairs on the porches, waving as they passed. A low bluff beckoned with a green meadow and shelter on the lee side and the weary travelers were thankful as a pair of wagons with folks around motioned them to join.

CHAPTER 5

ILLINOISTOWN

"Welcome, folks!" declared a portly man standing at the end of his wagon, his hand resting on the shoulder of a cheeky woman with a broad smile. He motioned to an area behind his wagon, "There's a good place right yonder!"

Eli grinned, waved, and with a nod to Benjamin, started to the edge of the trees just beyond a slight clearing with ample room for the wagon and team. The speaker and his wife followed them into the clearing, talking all the way. "We've been here most o' the day, stopped just 'fore lunchtime. Seems to be a right nice camp, water's nearby and good cover from the wind with that stand o' trees, an' it ain't too far into town if'n ya' need supplies."

Eli stepped down, extended his hand to the speaker, "Thanks for the invite. I'm Eli McCain and that's the Hamilton family. The young man is Benjamin, the mother Harriet, and the girls are Nora and Millie."

"I'm Luther Williams and this is my wife, Mildred,"

offered the speaker, extending his hand to Eli. Luther frowned, "Aren't you," nodding to the wagon, "together?"

"Oh, we just traveled the day together, just met up earlier and were goin' the same way," explained Eli.

With a glance to the wagon and the making-busy of the family, Luther answered, "Oh, I see. Well, the other wagon over yonder is a group of men headin' for the goldfields, not too friendly. Our son was killed in the war so we're going west for a new start, but our daughter, Maribel, is with us, she's been a big help," he explained, looking to his somber-faced wife. With another glance around, "Well, we'll let you folks get settled in, if we can help, just give us a holler!" The broad smile told of their sincerity and friendliness as they turned away.

"Thank you, folks," replied Eli with a nod and a wave. He led his horses to the little creek, loosened the girth as the big stallion dipped his nose in the cool water for a deep drink. Back to the edge of the trees, he stripped the gear from both horses, stacking the panniers and more beneath a wide spreading oak. He saw Benjamin leading the team to the water and after picketing his horses, he went to help the young man. As he neared, Benjamin looked at him, nodded, and said, "Ma's expectin' you for supper!"

"That'd be good, thanks," answered Eli, taking the leads of two of the horses as they started back to the trees.

As they picketed the horses, Eli noticed Benjamin looking to the other wagons, and turned to see what had attracted his attention. Eli smiled when he saw a young woman, who appeared to be about the same age as Benjamin, busy at the cookfire for her family, but not so busy as to not notice the young man who was new to the camp. Eli said, "Maybe you should go introduce yourself," grinning as Benjamin was visibly surprised when Eli's voice came out of the quiet.

"Uh, uh, how'd I do that?" asked Benjamin, looking a little embarrassed as he dropped his eyes to make busy with the horses.

"Oh, just walk over there with a big smile on your face and say, 'Hi, I'm Benjamin!'"

"I couldn't do that," he frowned, glancing from Eli to the other wagon.

"Sure, you can, Ben, nothin' to it! One thing you need to remember, time and opportunities are few and far between, so, now you have the time, and the opportunity is right there, so..." he nodded, spurring Ben to action.

With a nod and a tentative step, the young man started the short walk on the long journey that would surpass more time than any other short walk of his life. Eli stood, one hand on the rump of a horse as he leaned close to the animal and watched as Ben walked to the cookfire. He could not hear what was said, but the body language was obvious, and both were happy to meet. Eli chuckled and started back to the Hamilton wagon, remembering similar times of his own youth.

As he approached the cookfire where Harriet was busy with a Dutch oven, she looked up and saw the smile, which prompted one of her own, "What are you smiling about?" she asked. She put the lid on the cast iron pot and reached for the shovel to put some hot coals on the lid to cook the biscuits inside.

"Oh, just the folly of youth," answered Eli.

Harriet squinted her eyes showing suspicion and asked, "And just what might that be about?"

"Your son just walked over to the neighbor's wagon

to introduce himself to a cute young girl who was busy at the cookfire."

"He didn't," replied Harriet, doubting.

Eli chuckled, "He did, and you should be proud of him, he just grew up by about five years!"

"And just how much did you have to do with his 'growing up'?"

Eli chuckled, "I just encouraged him, that's all. Every young man needs encouragement every now and then. Don't you agree?"

Harriet cast a suspicious eye at their new friend, and answered, "Depends on the encouragement!"

"This used to be called Illinoistown," explained Eli, riding beside the Hamilton wagon. "Now they call it East St. Louis, that's St. Louis across the river there," nodding past the wide Mississippi River. Stretching for close to ten miles on the west bank of the big river, the burgeoning town of St. Louis marred the riverbank with docks, steamboats, packets, and the rising buildings beyond. The smoke from many stoves, furnaces, and boilers of the steamboats, hung like a low brownish grey cloud that made Eli think of the perils of the city that were many. He nodded ahead, "That's Wiggins Ferry landing and we'll take it across to the other side," nudging his claybank ahead. With the packhorse in tow, he dropped off the upper bank to the lower bank and went directly to the ferry landing. Stepping down, he flipped the reins of his horse and the lead of the packhorse over the hitchrail and stepped onto the boardwalk before the pay hut. He looked at the sign, shook his head and reached into his pocket as he stepped to the window. "One wagon, team of four horses, and two single horses."

"How many people?" asked the clerk, a bored expression wrinkling his face as he glared at Eli.

"Two adults, three young people."

"That'll be five dollars an' six bits," announced the clerk, watching Eli count out the money.

Eli gave the man six dollars in greenbacks and accepted a quarter in change, and the tickets. He walked back to the wagon, looked up at Benjamin, "Drive 'em onto the back o' the steamer there," pointing to the steam-driven ferry, "the crew will tie it down an' tell you where to put the horses. I'll follow after."

The ferry took two wagons, the Hamiltons' and the Williams', and the teams as well as both horses of Eli. As it moved from the landing, everyone took to the rail to look at the water and the approach to St. Louis. The big paddle wheel at the rear churned the water and the ferry moved through the ripples, all with a gentle rocking motion. The waves and the current pushed against the ferry, splashing onto the deck, but there was nothing disturbing about the movement nor the progress. Eli grinned as he watched the youngsters, the two Hamilton girls and Benjamin and Maribel standing side by side at the rail, talking, laughing, and pointing at the sights. Harriet came close to Eli, "I wish Cyrus were here, those kids are growing up so fast!" She wore a wistful smile as she spoke, glancing from Eli to the youngsters.

Luther and Mildred Williams stepped beside them, and Mildred asked Harriet, "Your son said you were going to Montana Territory, is that right?"

"Yes, we're going to join my husband there. He's building us a home," answered Harriet.

"Are you stopping in St. Louis?"

"Only to decide how we will go further, our friend,

Eli," nodding to Eli, "has said he will ask around about the best way—steamboat, wagon, or train."

"Oh, well, we'll be here a day or two, perhaps we could camp together?"

"Certainly, that would be nice. And where'bouts are you folks bound?"

Mildred looked at her husband and back to Harriet, "We're not sure. Just some place different to make a new start, away from so many memories," she answered, wistfully, accenting her words with a deep sigh.

"My husband has a profitable gold claim in Montana and said many are doing quite well. Perhaps you could try there?" but she paused, adding, "I don't mean to find gold, but where there's gold, there's people and people need to eat and that means farmers!"

Luther smiled at the thought, looking from Harriet to Mildred, "We might give that some thought." He leaned forward to look to Eli, "What way do you think best to make it to Montana, Eli?"

"Not sure, Luther, but I'll ask around. I'm not sure where I'll be going, but I can find out ashore. I'll see where you all are camped, then I'll ask around and let you know what I find," answered Eli.

"That would be helpful, sir, and we would appreciate any help you can give. I'm afraid these things are beyond me!" declared Luther, shaking his head.

"I understand. There was a time in the army that I had to make travel arrangements for hundreds of troops, so, I had to learn my way around some of these things."

It was but a short time later when the ferry was nudging up to the landing on the western shore, and the crew quickly freed the wagons of the many tie-downs and were directing the unloading. Once ashore, Eli led the way for the wagons to take the cobblestone Main

Street north to the edge of town and following the road, had a short distance to go before coming to an oft-used campsite where three other wagons were already camped, and horses grazed on some grass in a tree surrounded meadow.

CHAPTER 6

ST. LOUIS

Eli got an early start, up and on his way by first light, even though he knew most businesses would not be open until later, his plan was to inquire at those places where he thought his sons might have been or looked for work. His early inquiries when they passed through yielded a couple places, his first would be the stables and livery of Schulherr & Company on North Broadway. The doors stood wide open, and the morning light bathed the interior, revealing several stalls that harbored horses that were receiving their morning rations from a young colored boy who was busy with his pitchfork.

Eli stepped down, slapped the rein of his claybank around the hitchrail and walked into the wide doors. He called out to the boy, "You the boss man?"

The youngster looked wide-eyed at the big man, shaking his head, and answered, "No, suh, that be Massuh Hastings. He's o'er yonder," pointing with the pitchfork to a long row of stalls. Eli looked to see a big colored man who was also wielding a pitchfork and feeding horses. The man looked his way as Eli walked toward him. Eli asked, "Could I bother you a moment with a couple questions?"

The man glowered at Eli, stuck the tines of the pitch-fork into the dirt at his feet, and nodded. "What'chu want?"

Eli dug into his shirt pocket to extract the tintype showing his boys and walked closer to Hastings. He held it out for the man to see and asked, "Do you remember seeing those two men some time back. They're twins and might have been here looking for horses."

Hastings took the tintype and turned so the sun shone on the images. He glanced back at Eli and asked, "What'chu want 'em fo?"

Eli grinned, "Their mother—my wife—asked me to find them and bring them home."

Hastings relaxed his expression and nodded, "Sorry, can't 'member ever seein' the likes."

"Alright, thanks anyway. Also, I'm traveling with some folks that are headin' west and might be needin' to sell a team of four horses, and their wagon. Do you buy any horses?"

"I does that. They good team, used for anythin' but wagons?"

"They were used on a farm before coming this way. It's a woman and her children goin' to Montana Territory to join her husband. They'll probably be goin' by steamer, and it's too expensive to haul the wagon."

"I'll look at 'em, but don't need no wagon. But...muh neighbor," he nodded to the business just south of him, "is a wheelwright an' a wagon maker. He might buy it, but won't get top dollar from him, but prob'ly best you'll do."

"Sounds reasonable." Eli extended his hand to shake,

"My name's Eli McCain, and I thank you for takin' the time. When the family decides, I'll prob'ly come back with them and we'll make a deal."

"I'll be here," answered Hastings, nodding, and turning back to his work, but with a glance over his shoulder to watch Eli leave. He turned and took a few steps after Eli, and asked, "You wantin' to sell that saddle horse?"

Eli turned back, chuckling, "That'd be like selling a member of my family." With a glance back to his big stallion, he added, "He's more of a friend than anything. He's too good to sell and too faithful to part with."

Hastings came closer to admire the lineback red dun, walking around him, shaking his head and mumbling, "Sho would like to have me a stud hoss like that! Whooeee, I could make me some money off'n him, fo' sure'n certain!"

Eli chuckled, "He's bred a passel of 'em, back in Louisville where my wife's family had a horse farm. Raised Morgans and Tennessee Walkers. He's the best they ever had."

"If'n you change yo' mind, you come see me, ya' hear?"

Eli chuckled again, "Well, I might come see you again, but not to sell him." He swung back aboard the claybank and leaned down to stroke his neck, speaking softly in his ear, "You hear that, Rusty? That's another man that thinks you're a fine horse."

He pointed Rusty south, bound for the four hundred block of Main, but as he neared the town center, he found himself tasked with sidestepping and maneuvering around the horse-drawn railcars and the many hackney carriages and coaches. It was a busy town, and this was the beginning of a business day, and the many businessmen and office workers were hustling their way to work.

He soon found himself in front of the Merchants Bank on the corner of Fourth and Main Streets, but the only hitchrail was around the corner on the side of the building on Fourth Street. He stepped down, slapped the reins around the hitchrail and patted his stallion on the neck, assuring him, "I'll be back shortly. Try not to get into trouble!" He chuckled as he saw a passerby looking at him strangely as he talked to his horse, shook his head, and walked to the front of the bank.

Inside, at his request, he was ushered into the office of the president, Mr. Aldus Pinckney. The man stood as Eli walked in and after shaking hands, the president offered him a chair before the big desk and as they were seated, he asked, "And how may we be of service to you, Mr. McCain?"

"I would like you to transfer some funds from my bank to yours. I would like to have it more accessible as I will be in the West for a while and might have need of some ready cash."

"We would be happy to accommodate you, sir, and... are you of the McCains of Essex, shipbuilders and shipping?"

Eli grinned, "Yessir. That's my family. I'm surprised you know of our business."

"I'm from Baltimore and your family's reputation has preceded you. Is your father still running the business?"

"No, my father and mother passed, but the business is in capable hands while I'm away."

"Very good, now as to the transfer, if you'll just write down the details, we'll get it handled promptly and the funds should be available within the week." He pushed a paper and an ink pen in an inkwell toward him and continued, "If you need an advance, we'll be happy to accommodate you."

"That won't be necessary," answered Eli, sliding the paper back to the president. He watched as the banker's eyes widened at the sight of the number and when he looked up, Eli nodded. "If there's nothing else, I have some business to attend to. If you do not hear from me for some time, I will be traveling. I am in search of my sons—twins. We lost contact and would like to find them," he slipped the tintype from his pocket, held it for the man to see, and replaced it. "So, if you get a request or bank draft, it will be nothing to be alarmed about and I'm certain that amount," nodding to the paper held by the man, "will be more than sufficient."

When he rounded the corner to retrieve his horse, a scruffy-looking man was trying to get a grip on the reins but whenever he reached for them, Rusty bared his teeth and bit at him. The would-be horse thief started to raise a club to strike the stallion, but Rusty pulled back and reared up. Eli's habit was to just wrap the rein loosely around the hitchrail for just this reason, it gave the horse the freedom to loose himself and defend himself. The man staggered back, eyes wide, as he screamed and cursed at the stallion, but the horse, with nostrils flaring and teeth bared, was pawing at the air, and appeared to be spitting and glaring fire. As the man started to strike, Eli stepped behind him, grabbed the club and put the barrel of his Colt at the back of the man's neck, and said, "Drop it!"

The man froze, stammering and stuttering, watching the big stallion that now stood, prancing and snorting. Eli grabbed the club and pushed the man away, turning to face him and said, "Where I come from, we hang horse thieves!"

"Uh, I weren't gonna steal him, honest I weren't! I just wanted to pet him, he's a mighty purty horse, yessir!"

"Pet him with a club? Somehow, that's hard to believe. Now, do I summon a constable or are you gonna run an' hide?" asked Eli, grinning at the man's fright.

"I ain't gonna run, not with you pointin' that gun at me!"

Eli chuckled, cocked the hammer on the Colt, prompting the man with upraised hands to start back-stepping away as he stammered, "Don't shoot, don't shoot!"

Eli waved the pistol in a dismissing motion and watched the man turn and run. He mumbled to himself and Rusty, "Ain't got time to mess with the police. We got things to do!"

HIS NEXT STOP was just a couple blocks north on Main at the Folsom gun shop. They were well known and had been in business the longest and were considered one of the most reputable. His concern was more for information about his sons, but he was also shopping for ammunition and another weapon. When he stepped into the establishment, he paused a moment to take in the smell of gun oil, powder, leather, and more. It was familiar to the man that had spent so many years in the saddle with the cavalry from Fort Laramie to the battle of Appomattox Court House where he fought alongside General Phil Sheridan.

He stepped to the counter, looking at the weapons racked on the wall and saw what he was looking for, grinned, and motioned for the clerk. "Let me see that Colt shotgun, please."

The clerk looked at Eli, turned to retrieve the Colt Revolving shotgun and handed it to him. "Are you familiar with this weapon, sir?"

"I am. Some of my men used them in the last days of the war, and I determined to get one for myself." He looked it up and down, put it to his shoulder and sighted along the barrel, looked at the action and grinned at the clerk, "I'll take it, and a scabbard and I also need some ammunition for a Colt Army pistol and a Winchester repeater, both .44 caliber."

When the clerk sat the ammunition and rifle and scabbard on the counter and told Eli the price, Eli dug in his pocket for the money and asked the man, "Have you been here long?"

"This is my sixth year, sir," answered the clerk, smiling.

"Good, good. I have a question for you." He placed the gold coins on the counter, counting them out, then looked up at the clerk, "My sons might have been through here sometime in the last year or so," as he spoke, he retrieved the tintype, "and I thought you might look at this and see if they're familiar."

The clerk frowned, wondering about this man that asked about seeing someone as long ago as a year, but when he looked at the tintype, he smiled, looked up at Eli, "Twins?"

Eli nodded, "That's why I thought you might remember."

"I do," he paused, turned to motion to another clerk, and they both looked at the tintype, "Remember these two?"

The second man looked, glanced up at Eli and then to

the first clerk, "I do! They're the ones that bought all the Spencer ammo we had at the time. We didn't have much, but they took all we had. We thought they were gonna start another war when that Southerner asked 'em what they were gonna be fightin'!"

"Can you tell me anything about them, where they were going, anything?"

"They said they was gonna go to the goldfields in Indian country, but didn't say how or whereabouts exactly," answered the second clerk.

After giving his thanks to the clerks, Eli turned away and went to his horse, tethered in front of the store. His mind went to his sons, thinking about how they would go to the goldfields, and thought, *Maybe they're headed to the same goldfields as the Hamiltons, and probably by the riverboats.* He chuckled at the thought and swung aboard Rusty, pointing the big stallion to the waterfront.

CHAPTER 7

WATERFRONT

The brown cloud lay heavy on the big shoulders of St. Louis, fed by the foundries and factories, and added to by the many breweries that were earning their names in the burgeoning city, the greatest inland port of the growing nation. When Eli swung aboard his stallion, the stench of the sewage of the city rose from the gutters of the street and added to his motivation to make his visit to the city as brief as possible. Just a few blocks of hooves clattering on the cobblestones and Eli drew reins on the claybank stud, leaned forward on the pommel of his saddle, and took in the sight of the levee of St. Louis.

It stretched for six miles along the waterfront and was crowded with a variety of steamships and packets, several still emitting black smoke from the stacks that stood tall to mark the Hurricane deck of the many boats. Several were adorned with gingerbread and decorative rails, those that catered to passengers, while others stood utilitarian in their appearance, with nothing that was less than practical and purposeful.

The levee was littered with stacks of offloaded goods from bundles of products to bales of cotton and many unrecognizable items standing by themselves from farm implements to cannon. Burly stevedores and dock-workers pushed and shoved their way about, grousing about the many pickpockets and peddlers that sought to lift some money from passengers and crewmen alike. Off-key music rose from a variety of pretend musicians that struck discordant tunes from fiddles, organ grinders, squeeze boxes, flutes, and even a bagpipe. But the stench of the city and its sewage was displaced by the smells of stagnant water, dead fish, and unwashed bodies. Most of which was cast adrift by the breeze that pushed the waves and the ripples of the big river.

Eli shook his head, reached down to stroke the neck of his horse, "Rusty, that is the most confused pretense of organization that I have ever seen." As he watched, wagons and freighters were hustled to the stacks of goods, some looking for loads, others to empty theirs. All the while hacks pushed through the chaos to deposit their passengers, passing them off to the crewmen of the steamers and each being hopeful of picking up new passengers to transport to the luxury hotels of the city. Eli pushed ahead and dropped off the bank onto the sandy levee, knowing it was going to be a tiresome task to find out all he needed to know, both about his sons and the cost of passage to the northernmost port, Fort Benton.

He started at the south end of the almost six-mile-long levee. Stepping down and approaching the passenger plank, he looked for the captain or someone of authority, usually found by listening for someone barking orders. A man in a blue coat with brass buttons and a military-style hat with gold braiding, leaned over the rail from the upper Hurricane deck and hollered at a barrel-chested stevedore, "Jackson! Tell them others to get a move on, we need to be loaded an' outta here 'fore dusk!"

"Yassuh Cap'n," growled the man, mumbling less than flattering words that the captain could not hear but prompted Eli to chuckle and shake his head with a broad smile. Eli called up to the captain, "May I have a word, sir?"

The captain scowled as he looked at Eli, motioned him to come aboard an' growled, "Hurry up, ain't got all day!"

Eli ground tied Rusty, confident that the stallion would stay where he stood, even with all the strange noises, smells, and ruckus. Eli stepped quickly up the plank and took the stairs to the upper deck two or three at a time and stopped as the captain stood staring at him at the head of the stairs, "Alright, what'chu want? I ain't hirin' nobody, got muh crew!"

"I'm not looking for work, but I do have a couple questions," as he spoke, he retrieved the tintype and held it out before the man. "Do you remember seeing these young men sometime in the last year or more? They might have been looking for work or passage?"

The captain frowned as he looked at Eli and down at the tintype. He took the image and lifted it closer, catching the sunlight, and scowled as he looked at it. He looked up at Eli, "Twins?"

"Yes, that's my wife, their mother, between them. We lost touch and I promised their mother I'd try to find them."

"Can't say as I've seen 'em, course I only been runnin' the Mississippi for goin' on ten years, seen lots o' men, but don't 'member seein' them. Sorry." He paused and looked up at Eli, "You said you had other questions?"

"Yessir. I'm lookin' to go upstream, maybe to Fort Benton, and I need to know the costs for me and some friends, a family of four."

"Can't help ya. We just do the Mississippi; the Big Muddy boys are on the upper end of the levee. Might try the *Louella*, they're goin' upriver purty soon."

"Thanks, Captain," answered Eli, turning back to the steps. Over his shoulder he offered, "Have a good trip!"

He picked up the dropped rein and started walking along the levee, pausing by each steamer, and talking to the crew or captain, asking if they were going up the Missouri or Mississippi, and each would respond with "the Mississippi!" Most saying it with pride as if only the real steamships dared travel the big river. When he received repeated comments about the Big Muddy boys being further up the levee, he stepped back aboard his stallion and continued north. As he passed the many ships, he saw the names, some after sweethearts or other women of importance in the owner's life, like *Lillie Martin* and *Ida Stockdale*, while others were named after home ports or hometowns like *Dubuque Express* or *Fontanelle* and *Peninah*. Others took their names from famous leaders like *General Rucker, General Tompkins*, and *General Meade*. He also noticed a few unique names like *Far West, Yellowstone, Highland Chief*, and some named after Indian tribes, *Assiniboine*, and *Pawnee*.

His first positive response to the question of the Big Muddy prompted him to stop and step down. After tethering Rusty to the dock, he hollered up to the captain as he did before, and his results were the same. This action was to be repeated until he spotted the *Louella* whose crewmen were busy loading the big boat. He called up to the captain and was bid aboard. The captain introduced himself, "I'm Captain Grant Marsh, how may I help you, sir?" He appeared to be in his mid-thirties, dark brown but well-trimmed hair, a moustache that traced his upper lip as it dipped at the corners, yet a friendly expression and eyes that took in everything.

Eli extended his hand, "I'm Eli McCain," and before he could continue, the captain frowned and looked closer, "Of the McCain shipbuilders?"

Eli grinned, nodding, "Yessir, but that's not what I'm here about."

The captain nodded, "Continue, continue."

As Eli handed off the tintype, "I'm looking for those young men, they were through this area about a year or more past, that's their mother—my wife—between them. We lost touch and would like to find them."

The captain looked up at Eli, "And you're thinking they might have taken a ship upriver?"

At Eli's nod, he continued, "I don't recall having any McCains aboard, but there were a pair of twins…"

"Their last name is Paine. They're my stepsons."

The captain nodded, a smile beginning to split his face, "Ah, yes. They did come aboard. Worked as crewmen on a trip upriver." He frowned, adding, "I'm not sure if they went all the way, though. We had several crewmen jump ship near Fort Union. Don't remember if they were a part or not. I'd have to check my logbook."

"That won't be necessary right now, Captain. But I do have another question, there are two families I've been with that are considering taking a steamer to Fort Benton. They have family in the goldfield up there, and we need to know the cost and possibility of transportation."

The captain smiled, "We'll be leaving morning after

next, and as it looks now, we have a few cabins left and always have deck room."

"Would it be reasonable to ship wagons or not?"

"I don't think so. They take too much room and weigh too much to make it worthwhile and we don't have room to spare, too much cargo you see."

"And the cost?"

The captain pushed his cap back a little, scratching his head as he looked at Eli, "You look like a military man. Did you serve?"

"Yessir. I rode with Sheridan after my stint at Fort Laramie and other places."

"Then you can travel for half price, we might need your guns if we run into any Indian attacks like the Crow, Sioux, Assiniboine, Blackfeet, and more. But the rest," he reached in his pocket and pulled out a folded paper, a little worn around the edges, and showed it to Eli. "Those are the usual rates, cabins and such, as well as deck costs."

Eli looked at the figures, tallied them up in his head and looked back at the captain. "And do we pay this to you?"

The captain smiled, slowly shook his head, and pointed to the buildings that lined Water Street, "That white building there has the offices of the Fort Benton Transportation Company. They will provide you with the tickets, but if I were you, I would not wait, they can go quickly."

Eli smiled, "Understood." He extended his hand to shake and said, "We'll probably be traveling with you."

"Good! I'll look forward to getting better acquainted."

Eli quickly descended the steps, a renewed bounce in his step, swung aboard Rusty and spoke to his horse, "We're on their trail, Rusty!"

He paid for the tickets for himself, his horses and gear, and the Hamiltons with a bank draft, and took to the trail at as fast a pace as possible to share the news with Harriet and her family. He would have to let the Williams know, and help them, if possible, but he was pleased to have heard at least a little news about his sons. He was certain this was going to be a rewarding trip and would hopefully bring him and his stepsons together again. He looked heavenward and spoke aloud, "Thank you, Lord. Now guide me the rest of the way to my wayward sons, keep them safe and out of trouble in the meantime, and let their mother's wish be granted. Thank you."

CHAPTER 8

MISSOURI

"I made no contacts about a wagon train, but I did find out that my sons had been through here and took a steamer up the Missouri, bound for the goldfields," declared Eli, his face showing the good news with a wide grin. "I did talk to the captain of the boat they traveled on and he has a new boat that is leaving morning after next for another trip up the river to Fort Benton, Montana Territory. He said Fort Benton is the furthermost stop, unless they've made it to Helena, which is a bit further and where you're wanting to go."

"Oh my! That is good news for you, especially. I'm happy for you that you have some word about your sons." Harriet glanced around at her three children, and a quick glance to the Williams who had come to their wagon at the first sight of Eli.

"Does the boat have room for all of us?" asked Luther, pulling his wife Mildred a little closer, hope showing in their eyes.

"Yes, but you will need to get your tickets promptly while there are still cabins available," explained Eli, handing Luther a pamphlet showing the prices on the boat.

He looked back to Harriet, "I assume you might want to book passage as well?"

Harriet looked at Eli, back to her children and back to Eli, "It does seem to be the best way, but isn't it expensive? We don't have much, just the little that Cyrus sent."

"It is, but I also spoke with a livery and stable owner who said he might buy your teams and his neighbor is a wheelwright and might buy the wagon. Whatever you get for them would certainly help if not completely pay for your passage."

Harriet's eyes flared as she seemed to bounce with anticipation, looking back to the children who also showed excitement. With another glance to Eli, "Oh, that would be wonderful!" With a quick look to the setting sun, she added, "Would it be too late to talk to the man now?"

"Yes," answered Eli, but continued, "and there is much to do. You'll need to decide what you want to take with you, what you might sell to some of the others, or just leave behind. You are allowed baggage on the boat, but there's no room for things like furniture and such."

Luther stepped closer, lowering his voice, looking at the pamphlet, "I'm not sure we'll get enough to cover the whole cost of these tickets. Even if we do second class, it's still almost all we have."

"Let's worry about that after you make arrangements to sell the wagon and team, perhaps it will be enough," replied Eli. He turned his back to the others and spoke softly to Luther, "And if it's not, perhaps I can help."

"Oh, we could not ask you to do that!" exclaimed Luther, frowning. "If we can't get enough, we'll just make other arrangements, perhaps farm nearby." He lifted his eyes to the land that showed through the trees, "There appears to be good farmland here."

"Suit yourself, but the offer is there if you so decide."

Harriet stood and turned away, "Come on, girls, we must be busy about supper!"

Eli motioned for Benjamin to stay back and with an arm around his shoulder, they walked toward the horses, "Ben, I think it'll be up to you to make the deal with the livery and the wheelwright. You're the man for now, and I think your mother will agree. She'll have much to do here in camp, so we'll leave first thing to take the wagon and horses into town."

"Sure, Eli. I'd be proud to, but...you'll be there too, won'tchu?"

Eli grinned, "Yes, I will."

———

As HE FINISHED HIS COFFEE, Eli stood and motioned for Harriet to follow. He walked behind the wagon while Benjamin was busy with hitching the team and stopped, glancing around to be sure they were alone. He reached into his pocket and produced the tickets for their passage and handed them to Harriet. Her eyes grew wide as she looked at them, and back to Eli, "I don't understand!"

"I purchased them yesterday. I suspected you'd want to go, and I wanted to be certain you had passage." He saw her start to protest, and he held up his hand, "No, no, I know you're short on money, but perhaps the wagon and horses will make it up. If not, maybe your husband will have enough success with his gold claim to make up the difference. There's nothing to be concerned about, it'll all work out."

Tears welled up in her eyes, spilling out and coursing down her cheeks. She grabbed at a hanky in the pocket of her apron and wiped her face, nodding and trying to speak. She looked up at Eli, "You have been such a blessing. I thank the Lord often for bringing you into our lives at such a time. Thank you."

He dropped his eyes, looked back up at her from under his dark brow, and said, "This is just between us, understand?"

"Yes, yes, I do. And thank you, Eli. You are a great friend."

———

WITH A QUICK STOP at the levee to unload their baggage and let Harriet and the girls go aboard the riverboat to set up their cabins, Eli and Benjamin started for the Schulherr Stables and Livery. It was short work to sell the team and as Hastings summoned his neighbor to look at the wagon, it was also quickly sold. Eli had ridden his horse and brought along the packhorse. After a short negotiation, he purchased a saddle from Hastings and rigged the dapple grey. "Climb aboard, Ben," said Eli, with a wave to the horse.

Ben frowned, looking from the horse to Eli, "You're not..."

"No, I'm just letting you ride him for now. He's a good little horse, had him a while. He's a mustang from the mountains and surefooted as they come and more dependable as a watchdog than any dog you'll find!"

The young man smiled and swung aboard. Eli looked at Ben and asked, "I notice you been watchin' our back trail, lookin' for somethin' special?" He knew what the boy was looking for and could not help the grin that tugged at the corner of his mouth. Ben looked at Eli, shook his head, dropping his eyes in embarrassment, and chuckled, "Is it that obvious?"

"Yes, but it always is no matter how many girls you know," laughed Eli. "But I thought we'd ride back to the camp and talk to Luther and see what they've decided. We might be able to help 'em a little."

Ben smiled and reined the little gelding around to ride beside Eli. They had no sooner started back than they met the Williams driving their wagon toward them. Both men were smiling when they reined up before the wagon and Luther spoke, "Mornin'! We were hopin' to find you. Where's this ticket office for Benton?"

"I guess that means you've decided to join us?" replied Eli.

"Yessir. We thought about it, prayed about it, and believe that is the best opportunity for us."

"Good, good," replied Eli, and with a wave as he reined Rusty around, "Follow me!"

WITH TICKETS SECURED, they went to the boat to unload and let Mildred and Maribel go to their cabins. Luther followed Eli and Ben to the stables and wheelwright to sell the wagon and horses. As they finished their negotiations, Hastings looked to Eli, "You change yo' mind 'bout sellin' me that horse?"

Eli chuckled, "Nosir. I'm takin' him to Montana with me," and with a nod to the grey, "and that one too. They're my family!"

"An' a mighty fine fam'ly they is, too!" answered a chuckling and smiling Hastings.

———

THE *Louella* WAS CLASSIFIED as a packet because of its capacity to carry both cargo and passengers. She was a new boat, and this would be her first voyage up the Missouri. The stern-wheeler was built in McKeesport, Pennsylvania, and rated at 377 tons, measuring 200 feet by 30 feet by 4.6 feet, with double boilers. Ordered by Captain Jackman T. Stockdale, she was named after his daughter, Louella. Captained by the highly respected Captain Grant Marsh, she was piloted by Barnaby Nichols.

Eli and Ben secured the horses in the stalls on the first deck of the boat, as they would be the only animals on this trip. The rest of the deck would be used for cargo and deck passengers who would make their own spaces and provide their own food, usually cooking it aboard. It was the cheapest way to travel the river and many of those would be bound for the goldfields, full of dreams and ambition, but little money. They would also assist the crew whenever there was a wood stop, sometimes going ashore to cut the wood themselves and earn a little toward additional food and other accommodations.

Ben followed Eli up the staircase to the second deck, or the Cabin deck. With staterooms down both sides and the covered promenade walkway around the entire deck, it was the most commodious part of the ship. Staterooms had doors to the deck and to the interior cabin where the dining room lay between the rows of cabins. Most of the cabins were outfitted with two berths and a trundle bed under the lower berth, a dresser against the opposite wall, and a washstand with a washbasin and space for the ewer, or water pitcher. Each cabin had a chamber pot, a slop jar with handles on either side, the chamber pot being emptied once daily by the chambermaid. The toilet accommodations, one each for the ladies and gentlemen, was at the rear of the deck just forward of the big paddle wheel and the waste was emptied much like the typical outdoor variety, dropping directly into the river before the paddle wheel.

"So, what cabins do we have?" asked Ben as they topped out on the staircase.

"Let me show you, Benjamin!" said Nora, standing behind them. The girls had been waiting for their brother, anxious to show him around the boat. And it helped Ben to see Maribel with the girls, smiling coyly at the one she now considered to be her beau.

"They are so excited, I don't think they'll settle down until we reach Montana," declared Harriet, standing at the rail, her back to the forecastle, or bow of the ship, watching the girls lead their brother away.

Eli chuckled, "I take it this is their first time aboard a steamer?"

"It's my first time too!" declared Harriet, smiling broadly. Her smile faded as she looked at Eli, "Did the wagon and horses sell well?"

Eli grinned, "Very well. You won't have to worry about a thing. Oh, and I was thinking, since you only have tickets for one cabin, I have plenty of room and perhaps Ben could bunk in my cabin."

Harriet smiled, "There are only two bunks and a trundle in our cabin, and it would be better for him if he did not have to put up with his sisters."

"Then it's settled." He leaned against the railing, looking at the dock and the many roustabouts still busy with loading the cargo. He looked at Harriet, "Have you seen the main cabin, the dining room, yet?"

"I have! It is so luxurious! I certainly did not expect

that. And you said our meals are included with the tickets?"

"Yes, they are, and since this is a new ship, I suspect the food will be very good. They always want to make a good first impression." He looked about, frowned, "Have you seen the Williamses?"

"Yes, their cabin is on the far side of the main cabin, maybe a little further forward. Mildred was pleased and I think Luther was talking to the captain or someone."

"I wanted to talk to the captain before we left also, maybe I'll see if I can find them."

Eli tipped his hat to Harriet and started up the steps to the Hurricane deck where the long cabin housed the crew and supported the pilothouse atop. He was concerned about Harriet, fearful that she might be a little too lonely and looking for a close friend, but he was not about to let himself get any closer to her and the family than absolutely necessary for a pleasant journey for all.

CHAPTER 9

RIVER

The chuff chuff, clatter and clang, and hiss of the boilers spewed the grey and black smoke from the feathered smokestacks, as the whistle sounded its clarion call, and the engine began its chug chug to drive the long shafts and the massive paddle wheel began to turn. The splashing of the water gave its accompaniment to the sounds as the wheel began to churn, pulling the big boat back from the docks. As the current of the big river began to push, the stern of the boat moved with the current, but the pilot steered it clear, and the engine stopped for an instant until it began again, driving the big paddle wheel forward and pushing the craft against the current. The water at the wheel showed white, generating a bit of foam at the edge of the wake and the *Louella* was on its way. Another blast of the whistle bid goodbye to St. Louis as the northwestern-bound craft churned its way toward the confluence of the Big Muddy and the Mississippi.

Most of the passengers from the Boiler deck, or Cabin deck, were at the rail, many leaning out to look back at the paddle wheel while others stood looking about at the passing city of St. Louis and the limited scenery as the steamer chugged its way upriver. From the promenade, Eli leaned out a bit to look below at the many passengers on the cargo deck, most of whom were men, but he noticed a couple of women who held tight to their men, fear showing on their faces, whether from the new experience, or the very real threat to their safety and well-being among so many rowdy types. Harriet stepped near and exclaimed, "It *is* exciting!" she declared and added, "I never asked before, but how long will it take?"

"You mean the trip?" asked Eli.

"Yes, until we make Fort Benton or Helena."

Eli grinned, "The captain said it'll be about sixty days, give or take."

"Two months? Oh, my. Do we ever get off, you know, to go into a town or to at least walk on solid ground?"

"Well, there will be times when they stop for wood, and if there isn't any available, many of the crew and some of the passengers go ashore to cut wood and haul it back. So, I s'pose you could join a wood cutting crew." Eli fought to keep from chuckling and had to look away from Harriet when he said the last bit, afraid he would not be able to keep a straight face.

He heard her gasp and then push against him, bumping his shoulder with hers, "You're joshing!" she declared, giggling.

He chuckled and looked back at her, trying to show a stoic expression, "What? You don't think you'd make a good woodcutter?"

"Oh, I've cut more than my share of wood, but as far as this," responded Harriet, motioning to the lower deck and the stack of wood close to the boilers, "is concerned, I think there are quite enough men that are willing to work off part of their fare by cutting my share of the wood."

They felt the movement of the big boat as it made a slight turn to take to the Missouri and leave the vast reaches of the Mississippi. Their direction from the dock was almost due north, but now the Missouri River made a wide bend to the west and the south before turning back to the west. The clanging of the dinner bell summoned the cabin passengers to the main deck salon for the first meal of the day and the trip. It was at the captain's direction that the meals would be served what he called family style. The tables would seat eight people and would be tended by one server who also tended to two other tables. Luther and Mildred had already claimed a table and motioned for Eli, Harriet, and the youngsters to join them.

Their server offered both coffee and tea, as well as water and brandy. As soon as everyone had their drink, the plates full of food began to arrive. There were platters of eggs, sausage, bacon, biscuits, beans, potatoes, and a big pot of gravy. Harriet spoke before anyone filled their plates, "Could we have a prayer before we begin?"

Everyone looked around, nodding, until Harriet said, "Eli, could you ask the Lord's blessing on our day and our meal?"

"Uh, yeah, I s'pose," he answered, feeling a mite embarrassed, but remembering things from the past, he began and quickly finished with, "...and thank you, Lord, for your many blessings and this food. Amen."

The others echoed with their "Amen" and the food began to be passed around, much to everyone's delight. Luther was the first to say, "This is much more than I expected!"

Mildred smiled and said, "I could get spoiled by this.

Don't know what'll happen when I have to start cooking again. I might forget everything I know!" she chuckled as she elbowed Luther with a smile.

"Well, this might be a change, but nobody can cook like you," declared Luther, with a wink to Eli and a stifled chuckle.

The captain was making his way among the tables, speaking to the many passengers, and soon stopped at the table where Eli was seated. "Good morning, Mr. McCain. Are you finding the accommodations satisfactory?"

"Everything is fine, Captain." He nodded toward the others, "Let me introduce you, sir." He went around the table, giving each name as the captain nodded to each one. After he introduced Harriet, the captain asked, "And how do you like the meal?"

"Very good, Captain," replied Harriet.

"I changed things a little. Usually ships such as this have smaller tables and more servers, but since the war, workers are more difficult to find. Before and during the war, the riverboats often leased slaves from the riverside plantations, and we always had ample staff. But now, well, I thought this arrangement would make the meals friendlier, help folks get acquainted, and also need less staff."

Eli nodded to their server, "Jeremy has done a fine job. We couldn't ask for a better server." Eli looked up at the captain, "Our first stop?"

"Jefferson City, sometime Sunday afternoon."

Harriet and Mildred looked at one another, frowning, visibly counting the days and time, until Mildred exclaimed, "That's two and a half days away!"

"Yes, ma'am. Jefferson City is about a hundred seventy-five miles from St. Louis, by the river."

"Will there be services on Sunday?" asked Harriet.

"Perhaps. We do have a former military chaplain aboard, maybe we can encourage him to share with us on the Lord's Day."

"That would be wonderful, Captain. Thank you so much," responded Mildred, nodding to Harriet, and smiling at Luther.

When he finished his breakfast, Eli sat back, holding his coffee cup near his chin, as he looked about the main cabin. He saw at least three men that he pegged as professional gamblers as most riverboats attracted their sort, each thinking there would be several well-heeled passengers that could be fleeced. Four or five had the appearance of peddlers, probably bound for the goldfields to sell their goods. A few had the look of money men, probably investors looking for an opportunity to gain a share of the gold in the new find. Some appeared to be couples, like the Williamses and others, probably looking for their dream in a new land. One woman, although quite modestly attired, he guessed as a professional who would probably import other women once she established her place of business.

He finally spotted the man he guessed to be the former military chaplain, and he looked a little familiar. Eli chuckled, thinking to himself, *There will be plenty of time to get to know each one, including the chaplain, and see just how accurate my speculations are, probably all wrong, but it keeps things interesting*. He looked back at the chaplain, frowning, and beginning to remember.

It was the fall of '64, he was a major in the cavalry of the Army of the Shenandoah under Phil Sheridan. They were attacking a Confederate force under Jubal Early at Opequon Creek, near Winchester, Virginia. He led his company of cavalry into the battle, coming from the east, while others charged from the north. It was a bloody fight and Eli took a minié ball in his hip. It was enough to take him out of the fight and he woke up in a hospital tent, weak and bandaged, but after a quick check of his limbs, he knew he would be alright. It was then that a chaplain, named Milton T. Haney, came to his bedside, and offered to pray for him.

Eli responded, "Well, Chaplain, you're welcome to pray for me and if anyone needs it, I certainly do, but I'm not too sure the good Lord will recognize my name when you mention it."

The kindly chaplain smiled, took his hand, and said, "My son, my Lord knew your name before you did," and bowed his head and prayed for his soon healing. It was something that Eli would never forget, and he often thought about that, that the Lord knew his name before he did.

He shook his head at the memory, a smile tugging at the corner of his mouth and the action caught the attention of Luther who asked, "And what is it that makes you smile?"

Eli chuckled, "Oh, just a memory." He stood, pushed his chair to the table and looked around, "Excuse me, please. I think I see someone I remember from my past."

CHAPTER 10

CHAPLAIN

W hen Eli left the table, a glance over his shoulder showed everyone leaving, but he noticed Ben and Maribel start to the stairway together. He smiled and turned his attention back to the lone man sitting at the table. A newspaper was laid out on the table before him, and the man was focused on a particular story when Eli approached. He stood beside a chair and asked, "May I join you?"

The lone man looked up, his somber expression fading as he let a slight smile split his face and he motioned to the chair, "Of course, join me if you please."

Eli pulled out the chair, but looked at the man and extending his hand toward him, asked, "Aren't you Chaplain Haney?"

The man leaned back, surprise showing on his face as he slowly nodded, "Not a chaplain anymore, but yes, I'm Pastor Haney. Do we know each other?" he asked, accepting Eli's offered hand and shook hands as he was seated.

"I'm Elijah McCain, and it was at Winchester,

Virginia, 1864. Sometimes called the Third Battle of Winchester, or the Battle of Opequon Creek. We met in the field hospital in a local barn. I was wounded and you had prayer with me. You said something that day I'll never forget. When I said God probably wouldn't know my name, you said 'He knew your name before you were born.'" Eli paused as he leaned forward, elbows on the table, glancing down at the newspaper. Although it was not an oddity, it was a rarity, especially one from Chicago. He noted this was a copy of the *Chicago Tribune*.

Eli looked back up at the pastor as Pastor Haney asked, "And what did you do about it?"

Eli frowned, "Do about it?"

"Yes. Apparently, it was news to you that God knew your name before you did, so what did you do about it?"

"I don't understand."

"Whenever anyone learns something new, they have an opportunity to act upon their newfound knowledge. Whether someone tells them their shirt is torn, or they're being followed, or some new tidbit of wisdom, God allows us to know that new thought and expects us to act upon it. For example, when you found out that God knew you before you were born, did you bother to consider that and perhaps take a different direction in your life or maybe open His Word and learn more about the God who knows you so well?"

"Well, no, I did nothing...but I never forgot it!" declared Eli.

The pastor smiled and nodded, "Well, it's good to see you again, Elijah. Are you bound for the goldfields?"

"Uh, yes and no. I am helping a family that is going there to reunite with their husband and father, but I'm not going for the purpose of looking for gold. I am, however, looking for my sons—twins—that were last seen going that direction."

"Oh?"

Eli shared the story of his sons and the promise he made to their mother and the progress of his search thus far. The pastor listened closely to what he said, his facial expression showing his interest, but he made no comment about the search. When Eli finished his explanation, he asked, "And what about you, Pastor, are you heading to the goldfields?"

"Yes, but like you, I'm not looking for gold. I hope to start a church there. Maybe even minister to the Natives also. Not sure where exactly, but I am trusting the Lord to lead and to provide. It is a growing area and is definitely in need of the gospel."

"I understand the captain asked you to hold services here, come Sunday, is that right?"

"Yes, yes, he did."

"And are you?"

"Yes, I believe so. I look forward to sharing God's Word anytime and anywhere He gives me the opportunity."

Eli rose, extending his hand to shake again, "Well, Pastor. It's been good to talk to you again."

As they shook hands, the pastor asked, "And will I see you and your friends at the service Sunday?"

Eli smiled, nodded, and answered, "I'm sure Harriet and her children will want to be there and...I'll probably join them."

"Good, good," answered the pastor, smiling at Eli's discomfiture.

ELI LEFT THE SALON, taking to the promenade walk around the Cabin deck, wanting to locate Ben and Maribel. There was an uneasy feeling that stirred him, and he frowned as he looked about. Not seeing them on the cabin deck, he took the stairs down to the main deck. Cargo and firewood were stacked about, and the many deck passengers had claimed their spots by stacking their gear or bedrolls about. Roustabouts were feeding the furnaces with firewood, under the direction and supervision of the firemen. Wherever there was a flat spot on the cargo or deck, someone had lain their gear, making passersby negotiate their way among the many obstacles. Eli noticed a crowd gathering toward the bow of the boat, heard laughter and taunting, and quickly made his way toward the group.

A burly looking fellow was facing the bow but taunting someone before him. Eli got a quick glance of the couple before the man, it was Ben and Maribel, facing him. The agitator said, "Now looky here, sonny, there ain't 'nuff women to go 'round an' folks gotta share. So how 'bout you just go on back to where you came from an' leave the little woman here with us'ns?" He cackled as he stretched out as if to grab the young woman.

He was stopped by a voice behind him, "Didn't your mama teach you any manners?"

The man growled as he turned, lifting his arm as if to strike. He saw a figure behind him and spun around, but Eli caught the man's right wrist in an ironlike left-hand grip and jerked him forward, burying his right fist in the man's belly, bending him over. He dropped to his knees, wincing at the pain, but struggling to free himself. He brought up his left fist, attempting to strike Eli in the jaw, but Eli brought the man's arm down, striking the deck with his elbow and making the man drop his head. But before he could react, Eli jerked him to his feet, backhanded him, slapping and backhanding his face repeatedly, driving the man to his knees again. The raucous crowd hollered, cheering them on, but stepping back and giving them room, with some even shouting about making bets. Eli, with his grip still on the man's right wrist, jerked him to his feet, turning him around and twisting the man's arm behind him. Eli said, "This is your first lesson in manners. Always respect a woman!"

Eli shoved the man to the railing and grabbed the seat of his britches and lifted him and shoved him overboard. The ruffian screamed as he sailed through the air, splashed into the water, spitting, fussing, and kicking. The crowd cheered, jeered, laughed, and shouted until Ben shouted, "Behind you!"

Eli heard someone behind him and quickly turned, catching another man who was about to club him with a big piece of firewood. He was a young man, maybe the same age or a little older than Benjamin, but he growled, "That was my partner! He can't swim!" Eli had grabbed the man's wrists above his head, and with that iron grip, slowly brought the man's arms down, forcing him to drop the big stick. The man went to his knees as Eli looked at Ben, "Hand me that board," nodding to a board lying at the top of a crate, probably a part of some other crate. Ben did as he was asked and handed Eli a board that measured about four inches wide and thirty inches long. Eli jerked the young man to his feet, spun him around and bent him over his knee and began to paddle him. The young man hollered, screamed, and kicked, all to no avail as Eli delivered swat after swat. The crowd began to applaud, laughing and jeering. Finally, the young man whimpered, motioning to the rail and his partner, "He'll drown!"

The mate was attracted by the ruckus and pushed his way among the crowd, barking at the roustabouts and directing them back to work. As the crowd began to thin out, the rest fell silent, watching. Eli lifted the young man to his feet, allowing him to pull up his britches and step closer to the rail. Eli nodded to the water and the young man's partner, "Where he landed, that water is no more than four feet deep. All he has to do is stand up—if he's smart enough to do that." The young man whimpered some more and went to the rail, looking for his partner. Eli was behind him and asked, "You wanna join him?"

"No," he grunted, shaking his head. "But all his stuff's here."

"That's the price of bad manners," stated Eli. "But all he has to do is catch the next boat and you can wait for him at the next stop."

"But he has no money," pleaded the young man.

"Then he might get another new experience. He'll just have to earn his way by working." Eli shook his head as he turned away, motioning to Ben and Maribel to come with him as he started to the stairs. With a last look at the young man at the rail and the disbursing crowd, they mounted the steps and went to the rail on the promenade, thoughtful about the happenings.

CHAPTER 11

PROMENADE

"I didn't expect that!" declared Benjamin as he leaned on the railing, looking at the water as the big boat churned its way upstream. The shore was thick with trees, cottonwoods, maple, oak, and willows—all shielding the passing boats from view. Ben turned to look at Eli who stood, his back to the river as he leaned on the rail, looking sidelong at Ben and Maribel. "We just wanted to see the rest of the boat," he pleaded.

"Well, a lesson learned is never a waste of time. It's a good thing to know that not everybody you encounter has the same values as you've been taught. Although in most places, all women are greatly respected, but all too often there are a few men that haven't learned their manners."

"Well, you certainly taught them!" declared a smiling but very relieved Maribel.

Eli looked at the girl, "Just remember what you learned today. Don't go anywhere unaccompanied, it's just not safe. And when we get to the goldfields, you'll find that doubly so for there are many men that have long been without the company of women, and they can easily get out of hand."

Maribel frowned, "Are the Natives the same way? I mean, do the men respect their women or..." she shrugged, unable to put into words the many thoughts that flooded her mind.

Eli turned to face the girl, "Maribel, Ben, you'll find that people are basically the same wherever or whoever they are, I mean, whether they are Natives, whites, colored, or others, there are good and there are bad. I've been among several different native peoples and found most of them honorable and respectful, in their own way of course. Their way of life is different than ours, but that does not make it better or worse, just different. And likewise with coloreds, you'll find the same thing with them. Their mothers especially, teach them manners and respect and more, but there are some that turn out bad, just like those white men you just encountered."

He looked from Maribel to Ben and continued, "I reckon what I'm saying is, don't let the externals, you know, the color of their skin, the clothes they wear or the way they speak, be all you measure about a person. I've seen some well-dressed, well-spoken, dapper types that you couldn't trust any further than that rowdy I threw overboard. And I've also known some that wore ragged clothes, had difficulty expressing themselves, and were unaccustomed to the way of people, but were fine people and the kind I'd prefer to have on my side, even more so than some of the others."

"That was a fine sermon, Elijah. Maybe you should preach the Sunday service."

The voice came from behind Eli prompting him to turn and see Pastor Haney standing at the rail and smiling. Eli shook his head, chuckling, "I didn't know you were there, Pastor. If I had, I would have turned the pulpit over to you!"

Eli turned back to Ben and Maribel, "Let me introduce you to a friend of mine." He turned back to the pastor and introduced the two young people and after the usual cordial greetings, Eli excused himself, "I think I'll go for a bit of a walk around the deck." He glanced down at the newspaper under the pastor's arm, "When you're done with that, I'd like to read it, if you don't mind."

"Of course, here," he replied, handing the paper to Eli. "I've about read the writing off the pages so you might as well have a go at it."

"Thanks. It's been a while since I've had the opportunity to take my time and browse through the news and such."

"Enjoy!" stated the pastor, turning back to the rail, leaning on his elbows to watch the passing water and the less than scenic shoreline.

Eli turned away and started to the aft, ambling along the promenade walkway, occasionally stopping at the railing to look below and across the ripples to the shore. He stood at the rail and watched the churning of the big paddle wheel, driven by the long shafts from the engine, always moving, keeping the boat charging against the current. The pilot and captain kept a sharp lookout from the pilothouse, one on the wheel, the other with field glasses at the window, watching the channel and keeping the big boat in the deepest part. Although the *Louella* had a draft of less than four feet, there were sweepers, sandbars, and snags that could bring it to a sudden stop. Occasionally the mate would take a sounding and call out the numbers to the pilothouse, but he was at the bow of the boat and could not be heard above the engines and paddle wheel as it churned its way through the muddy waters.

Eli turned away from the big wheel and ambled along the promenade, making his way to his cabin door. He grabbed a deck chair and sat down, stretching his feet up onto the rail and unfolded the newspaper. He quickly scanned the headlines, noting especially the column headed by the bold print **CONGRESS**. The subtitle was *The Reconstruction Resolutions in the Senate.* Eli shook his head, thinking, *We just fought a war and over a half million men lost their lives for this very reason, and now the politicians want to make more laws about the very thing we fought for!* He had done his best to stay informed about what was being called "reconstruction." But this article was about the Thirteenth, Fourteenth, and Fifteenth Amendments, and the politicians were debating about the Thirteenth that abolished slavery, the Fourteenth that gave citizenship rights and equal protection under the law, and the Fifteenth was about the right to vote. He shook his head knowing that every man that wore blue and fought in the war was fighting for those very things and now the politicians were fighting among themselves whether to make these principles into amendments to our constitution. He shook his head, disgust showing on his face, as he turned his attention elsewhere on the paper.

He noted articles that detailed how the Presbyterians and Methodists were being disagreeable about policies and procedures, North Carolina and Ohio were fighting among themselves, and Europe was in the beginnings of financial panic. He shook his head, looked across the page and chuckled as he read advertisements for Roback's Bitters and Blood Purifier Blood Pills and if that didn't work, there was an advertisement for Dr. Lighthill's remedies to cure deafness and blindness and asthma. He laughed at the advertisement for Dr. Winchell's Teething Syrup and Eilert's Daylight Cathartic Pills.

Well, if the politicians can't agree on anything, maybe we better send them all a good supply of these wonder pills!

He finished scanning the paper, dropped his feet to the floor, and folded the newspaper as he stood. But a hail from the captain stayed his leaving and he waited for the man to join him at the rail. "Glad I caught you, Eli. I have a favor to ask."

"Ask away, Captain. If I can do it, consider it done," answered Eli, lifting his foot to the lower rail, and leaning on the top rail with his elbows.

"We'll be stopping about dusk at a place called Hog Hollow. There're usually some wood hawks there and we'll be needing a few cords. But there have been times that pirates or outlaws have tried to board us, steal some cargo, you know, such like. And I'd be pleased if you'd take a place at the rail, rifle in hand, just to discourage such. Would that be asking too much?"

"Of course not, Captain. I can always use a little target practice."

"It's easy to tell the workers from the shirkers and there's no need for any of the wood hawks to come aboard. My roustabouts will do the loading and you can spot them when we stop and lower the gangplank. Probably won't have it here, but further upstream, there are some Natives that have gotten pretty sly and try to get the boat to stop to trade. I've even known 'em to wade out into the water, crouch down to make it look like the water's deep, maybe up to their shoulders or more, and wait for the boat to ground itself. Then they stand up and try to get aboard. Heard about that happenin' to a boat last fall, they took everything, killed the crew, and burnt the boat!"

"Are we just stopping for wood or are we spending the night?"

"No, the moon is waxing gibbous, or about three-quarters, so we'll have enough light to steer by, so we'll make time while we can. It'll be about suppertime, so if it is, I'll have Cooky set aside your supper, keep it warm."

"I'd appreciate that. I think I'm going to get spoiled, having regular meals and such. Even in the army, 'fore the war, didn't have that. Out on patrol too much."

The captain tapped Eli on the shoulder as he moved away, smiling, and offering a thanks over his shoulder. He had to return to the pilothouse and take the wheel as the pilot took his turn at watching for snags and sandbars.

CHAPTER 12

WOODHAWKS

The boat nosed into the sandy shore on the eastern point of a timber covered island. The sun was barely peeking above the western horizon as dusk began to lay its comfortable blanket of muted light upon the land. It was the softer time of the day, even the birds seemed to be settling in for the coming night and the ripples of the river quieted their usual angry retorts and began to lend a melodic background to the cool of the day.

The captain stood beside Eli at the rail on the Cabin deck, looking down as the roustabouts stretched out the gangplank and others heeded the barked orders of the mate as they tied off the boat, fore and aft, with the long, braided ropes. He turned to Eli, "We'll be loading about sixty cord, it'll take a while, but we'll prob'ly be tradin' some goods for the wood as well as money. So, you might see a couple of their men goin' to the hold and carryin' out things. One thing I won't trade, is the casks of whiskey, they're worth too much at the end of the line. So, if you see anyone trying to take a cask, stop 'em."

Eli chuckled, "I understand, Captain, but that won't make you very popular with the wood hawks."

"I'm not worried about my popularity, just getting my cargo to its destination. We've got a variety of goods, from whiskey to plows and books, and I want it all to get to the end of the line."

There were at least four dirty and burly men standing by the massive stack of wood that lined the shore, waiting for the work to begin. Another man stood, hands on hips, as he watched the tie-off and looked to the boat, searching for the captain. This was the man that would make the deal for the wood and with a glance over his shoulder to Eli, Captain Marsh started down the stairs, to make his way to the gangplank and do the bartering for the wood.

Just for appearances, Eli stood at the rail above the gangplank, rifle cradled in his arms, watching all the activity. The boat had been pulled tight against the shore, allowing more planks to be dropped and the loading to begin. Starting as close to the stern and the furnaces as space would allow, the men stacked the wood four square and six foot high, two squares deep and the long stack of wood creeped forward, with the hardest part of the load being the water side, causing the men to carry the wood to the far side of the boat. If the grumbling and complaining could be harnessed, the work would go faster, but hardworking men reserved the right to snivel and gripe. The roustabouts from the boat did the work on board and along the gangplank, but the work on shore was done by the wood hawk crew.

It was nothing more than good-natured banter between the crews, often chiding one another about how quickly they could stack the wood and more. But when one big man of the wood hawk crew threw one of the four-foot pieces of wood at a roustabout, catching him with his back turned and knocking him off the plank and into the water, the temperament of the workers changed. The roustabout slogged out of the water and started up the plank, until the wood hawk chided, "Now that'chu got a bath, mebbe you'll catch up wit' the rest of us!"

The roustabout was probably the biggest of the boat's crew and he stopped dead still, his back to the shore and Eli watched as the man pulled his hands into fists, squinted his eyes, and grew tense all over. He glanced to his shipmates, and slowly turned around, glaring at the talker. He stomped down the plank, his shoulders bunched and his back slightly bent, resembling the fighting stance of an ape, and growled, "Mebbe you need a bath, boy!" and charged the big man.

The roustabout, known only as Mac, barreled into the wood hawk, his shoulder slamming against the man's chest and driving them both to the ground. They separated and came to their feet, both in a crouch, hands at their sides, and charged one another and the fight was on, prompting the other workers, both roustabouts and wood hawks, to gather around and cheer on their man.

The captain was on the main deck, near the forward gangplank and turned to look up at Eli. Cupping his hands to his mouth, he hollered, "Let 'em fight it out! Just try to keep 'em from killin' each other!"

Eli nodded and turned his attention back to the fight. The wood hawks were cheering their man, Smitty, and the roustabouts cheered on Mac. The men appeared to be well matched, until they stood toe to toe and began slugging it out. Eli knew boxing, having done some at West Point, and after graduation he trained some with Tom

Allen, the British boxer that settled in America and fought the circuit from St. Louis to New York. Eli watched Mac who had taken the measure of his opponent and often dodged the bigger man's swing and answered with a volley to the man's middle, the damaging blows soon taking their toll.

It was when Smitty brought a roundhouse swing to the head, hoping to flatten Mac, that the roustabout slipped under the slamming right, buried his left fist in Smitty's middle and followed that with a flurry of punches to his kidney. Smitty bent in the middle and fell on his face, rolling to his side, his hand at his ribs. Mac had broken at least one of his ribs and it brought excruciating pain to the big man. He had never been bested by anyone on the waterfront and he was angrier than he was hurt. He rolled over and struggled to his feet, while Mac had turned away, thinking the fight was over.

Smitty glowered at Mac's back, turned, and grabbed one of the lengths of wood and lifted it overhead, charging toward Mac. Eli had lifted his rifle to his shoulder when he saw the wood hawk grabbing at the pile and as Smitty lifted the big stick, Eli fired. The bullet split the wood, knocking it from the man's hands and causing every man to look to the boat to see Eli jacking another round into the chamber. He raised his voice just enough to be heard, and asked, "Who's next?"

The men were frozen in place, until the Mate hollered, "Let's get that wood aboard! We're wastin' daylight!"

The shouted order pulled the pin on the stoic and still workers and each man returned to the task at hand. As the stack on shore dwindled, the boat slowly dropped in the water. With sixty cords loaded, Eli took the stairs and went to the main deck. The wood hawks had come aboard, and their leader was directing them as they went to the hold for their traded-for supplies. Eli leaned against the stack of wood, watching the workers pack out their goods. One man, at least as wide as he was tall, had a cask on each shoulder, his head lowered as he moved to the plank. But Eli stepped in front of him, causing him to look up, wide-eyed at his impediment. "Uh, can'tchu see I'm loadin' stuff?"

"Not that," replied Eli, smiling at the man.

"You want me to drop this on yo' head?" growled the man, scowling at Eli.

"You'll need to grow about a foot 'fore you can *drop* it on my head," answered Eli, but he continued, "Now, how's about takin' it back to the hold and getting something your boss actually traded for?"

The man growled, "Git outta my way!"

Eli smiled, stepped back a little, turned slightly away as if he was getting out of the way, but with a slight turn, he drove the butt of the rifle into the man's middle, bending him over and loosing his grip on the casks. Eli quickly grabbed the nearest cask, setting it down and grabbed for the other, but it hit the deck and started rolling down the plank. A roustabout saw the rolling whiskey cask and gave chase, but when the cask rolled off and into the water, he dove in after it. Unfortunately, the water was shallow and both cask and roustabout almost buried themselves in the wet sand, but the man came up first, sputtering and spitting, wiping his eyes free of water and sand. With a quick look around, he saw the cask sitting askew and grabbed at it. He shouted to the lookers-on, "I got it!"

Eli laughed at the man in the water, watched the big man at his feet struggle to his feet, and motioned with the muzzle of his rifle for him to go ashore, which the big man did, grumbling all the way. The rescuer of the whiskey cask lifted it free from the sand, set it down on the plank and hoisted one leg then the other to join his round companion. He stood, looked up at the deck to see the captain watching, and asked, "Since I rescued it, don't that make it mine. You know, under the salvage laws of the river?"

"Only if you share it with the rest of the crew," answered the smiling captain, "but not until we have a layover! There's too much to be done this night, we're travelin' by moonlight." And it was by the moonlight that the steamer *Louella* backed away from the sandy shore and took to the current of the Missouri, or Big Muddy, River. The captain, now at the wheel in the pilot-house, had invited Eli to join him. He turned to his guest and asked, "You ever pilot a riverboat?"

Eli chuckled, "Nope, don't want to either!" he declared, looking to the moonlight bouncing off the waves before them. The ripples juggled the jewels of starlight, while the prow of the big boat pushed aside the waves that carried the image of the moon before them. Eli looked along the shoreline that held nothing but deep shadows and darkness and he could not help but think what kind of evil the darkness might hold. He shook his head and returned his gaze to the meandering river, watching the captain spin the wheel about and bark orders through the pipe to the engineers below. He smiled as he remembered the many times he was the one in charge and barked orders to his many junior officers and troopers in his command.

CHAPTER 13

TWINS

"What'cha thinkin', Jubal?" asked Joshua, looking over the low fire to his brother who looked like he was brooding or at least in some distant place with his usual mind travels.

Jubal, the younger of the twins and the more guarded or quiet of the two, looked up at his older brother, and picked up a stick to stir the coals of the cookfire. Strips of meat overhung the coals, dripping fat juices into the fire that sizzled and snapped. "Oh, not much. Just wonderin' if Ma got any of our letters and how she's doin'. Wonderin' if Pa got home to her and what he's thinkin' 'bout us desertin'."

"Won't do no good wonderin'. We can write again when we get settled somewhere an' mebbe she can write back and let us know 'bout things," suggested Joshua, knowing the melancholy moods of his brother that always stood in contrast to his short temper. "Leastwise, since the war's over an' we been gone so long, I doubt if the army's lookin' for us. So, if we ever decide to go back home, we can."

Jubal tossed the stick into the flames and stood. He glared at his brother, "I ain't interested in goin' home, unless our pockets are lined with money, or gold nuggets! Then we can strut and spend and find all the girls that wouldn't have anything to do with us a'fore!"

Joshua frowned at his brother, "You mean to tell me the only reason you're doin' all this is cuz you wanna show MaryLou how wrong she was when she called you a loser?"

"I ain't no loser!" growled Jubal, glaring at his brother, eyes flashing with the fires of anger.

"I know, I know! Settle down!" cautioned Joshua, carefully watching his normally quiet brother, knowing how easily he could lose control.

Jubal stomped around the camp for a moment, glancing to the other small cookfires along the line of freight wagons. He shook his head and returned to his seat. He picked up one of the willow branches that held a strip of meat, looked closely, and replaced the stick for the meat to finish cooking. They had been working for Paquette Freight Company for several months and the freighters were bound for Dauphin Rapids on the Missouri River where they would ferry freight from the riverboats that couldn't make the rapids, to Fort Benton and Helena. The brothers had signed on when their boat offloaded their cargo, and the freight company was short-handed. It appeared to be the opportunity they wanted. With intentions of making it to the goldfields, it appeared to be the answer they sought. Each freight wagon carried a crew of four who alternated driving and securing the loads as well as keeping watch for outlaws, renegades, and raiding Indians.

"So, is our meat 'bout ready?" asked Pug Witcher. He was the senior member of their crew having been with the company for more than three years. He was a middle-aged man with a circle of hair that framed his bald pate and a rolled belt that resembled his hairline as it fought to keep the man's big belly under control. Pug was always hitching up his pants and snapping his galluses as he leaned back while he talked. "I'm 'bout ready to eat a whole buffler!" He cackled at his own try for humor, looked at his partner, "How 'bout'chu Whittaker?"

"I'm always hungry!" grumbled the long, lanky sour-puss whose britches were held up with one wide strap of woven leather that angled across his chest and over his shoulder. His canvas britches, always dirty and holey, had rolled up cuffs that showed his hobnail boots. Whittaker seldom talked and when he did it was usually about food. His only whiskers were a few at the point of his chin and were not easily seen due to the camouflage of dirt and drool.

Joshua nodded to the meat, "Go 'head, grab a stick. There's cornbread in the dutch oven and coffee in the pot."

As the men poured themselves some coffee and grabbed a cornbread biscuit, all but Whittaker put the meat in the biscuit and began to eat. Whittaker chose to eat the meat off the stick, alternating bites with the corn-bread. With the meat juices running down his chin, he paid no attention as it dripped into his open shirt and slid down his hairless chest. Jubal noticed the drips, shook his head, and moved away from the man just as the evening breeze carried the stench of his unwashed body toward Jubal, prompting a sour facial expression as he glanced toward Whittaker.

"Whittaker, we've made four trips, this is number five, together. And in all that time, I've never seen you even wash your face. When was the last time you took a bath?"

"Why would I do that?" he asked between bites of juicy meat.

"Because you stink! And your smell is ruinin' my supper!" declared Jubal, shaking his head.

"You ain't no posey," drawled Whittaker, unwilling to pause his eating.

Jubal looked at the others, "Maybe what we oughta do when we get to the river is to throw him in and toss him a bar of lye soap."

"In the Missouri? It's dirtier than he is. Won't do no good," answered Pug, grinning at his partner.

"Better yet, we have to cross the Judith in a day or two, it's clean, and maybe that'll work," suggested Jubal.

"Nope," answered Whittaker, still eating.

"Why not?" asked Jubal, frowning at the man.

"Knowed a man onct. Never took a bath. His friends threw him in the water, scrubbed him clean. Two days later he was dead. Caught his death, he did. Nope, ain't gonna do it!" declared Whittaker, reaching for another piece of meat. "Sides, if'n you was to try, I'd hafta skin you like I done that buffler." He glanced to Jubal, his expression not threatening, just a matter of fact.

Jubal shook his head, eyebrows raised as he looked at the others, "Well, it's a good thing we ran into that herd today. That buffalo meat will last us a good while." It was his way of changing the subject, but not dropping the thought of an unsolicited bath for the stinker.

———

THE TWINS WALKED TOGETHER along the bank of the narrow creek, dusk had settled over the land and the sounds of the night prevailed. Jubal asked, "What're we gonna do?" looking to his brother. Their original plan was to make it to the new gold strike in a place called Alder Gulch, but with little money and no supplies, they had determined to work for the freighter until they could outfit themselves and seek out a gold claim. But those plans had been waylaid by circumstances and pay that seemed to evaporate as quickly as it was earned.

"Well, we've got a little set aside, but not enough to outfit us. If we could find something that pays a little better, or even something in the goldfield, maybe working for another claim..." mused Joshua, shaking his head and reaching for a stick to toss into the dark. As he came erect, he cocked his arm back and threw the stick toward the bushes that lined Arrow Creek, "If only..."

"If only what?" asked Jubal, dropping to his haunches, and watching the moonlight bounce off the waves of the creek.

"If only we could get money from home. You know Pa's family has money, and so does Ma's. But we can't tell 'em where we are, leastways not now. Even if we weren't deserters, there's no way we could get money from 'em," explained Joshua, kicking at the cones at the base of a piñon tree.

"Look, we'll get paid after this trip. If there's any cargo for Helena, that'll put us right where we need to be, and we'll have enough to at least get a few supplies, and maybe we can get work in the goldfield, you know, helping build sluice boxes, or waterways, or..." shrugged Jubal.

"Yeah, maybe, but...I dunno, there's just so much freight and such. It'd be easy to set some aside and make money."

Jubal frowned, scowling at his brother, "We may be deserters, but we ain't thieves!"

"Not yet."

———

"WHAT'S HIS STORY?" asked Barnaby Nichols, the pilot. He was busy at the wheel as the captain scanned the water, and Eli had come up the stairs from the Hurricane deck and was nearing the pilothouse.

The captain looked where Barnaby had nodded, grinned back at his pilot, "He's lookin' for his sons. They took passage, well, worked for it, last fall on our last trip up the river on the *John J. Roe*. You might remember, they were twins, young men, dark brown hair, Jubal and Joshua."

"Yeah, I remember them. Good workers, but if I remember right, I think they got off when we offloaded freight so we could make Dauphin Rapids. You remember, the freighter, uh, I think it was, uh, some French name, Packet? No, Paquette! They usually have freighters at the rapids."

The captain frowned, looking at his pilot. When Eli rapped on the door of the pilothouse, the captain motioned him in and shook hands when he entered. "Mornin' Eli. We were just talkin' 'bout'chu. Barnaby here remembers seein' your boys get off the boat this side of Fort Benton at a place called Dauphin Rapids. It's a place where some boats hafta stop and offload some freight to get over the rapids. Some of 'em double trip it to pick it up, but others just let the freighters take the load on ahead to Fort Benton and such."

Eli looked at the pilot, "You remember 'em, huh? Do you remember what they did when they got off?"

"Well, usually any crew that jumps ship there, joins up with the freighters. They're always lookin' for help, what with so many of their bullwhackers quittin' for the goldfields."

Eli looked at the captain, "Where do the freighters usually go?"

"If the captain of the boat allows it, they'll take the freight on to Fort Benton, sometimes on to Helena, depending on the freight."

Eli slowly lifted his head, pursing his lips, thinking about the twins.

The captain interrupted his thoughts, "But if you're wanting to find them, you'd do better by staying aboard until we get to the fort. It'll be faster and you'll probably find out more from the freighters at the fort."

Eli nodded, turned to look at the river, his mind chasing thoughts of the twins and the many possibilities, but he allowed that he knew more about them now than he expected when he set out on this journey. The possibilities were promising, and he could still be a help to the Hamiltons and the Williamses as he had promised.

CHAPTER 14

PROGRESS

It was approaching dusk on the fourth day when the boat nosed into the bank beside the long stacks of wood readied by the Woodhawks. Eli chose this stop for a brief time ashore for his horses and as soon as the boat was secured and the gangplank dropped, he led Rusty and the packhorse, both saddled, down the plank with Benjamin following behind. Once ashore, they mounted up and started for the trees. A trail split the trees and pointed away from the town of Boonville, offering a good place for the horses to stretch their legs. Within moments, the trail broke from the trees and joined a wider roadway that paralleled the river, giving the riders room to ride side by side.

"So, how you likin' the travel on the riverboat?" asked Eli, looking to his younger charge.

"It's somethin', it surely is. Never thought I'd see the day when we'd be travelin' on a riverboat," replied a smiling Benjamin.

"Which do you like better, travelin' on the riverboat or bein' close to Maribel?" chuckled Eli.

Ben dropped his head, slowly shaking it side to side, before looking up at Eli, "Uh, I don't rightly know how to answer that. She's mighty pretty and I like bein' with her, but..." stammered Ben, shrugging.

Eli chuckled, "She is pretty and she's a nice girl. You two make quite a pair, and since your families are goin' to the same place, you might be near one another for some time. How old are you now, Ben?"

"I'll be sixteen in a couple months," declared the boy, his chest expanding as he sat straighter in the saddle.

"Well, you're still young, although there were several in my company that weren't much older, and I've known some that got married at that age, girls mainly."

"Married!?" replied a startled Ben, looking wide-eyed at Eli. "Nobody said nuthin' 'bout gettin' married!"

"Don't go gettin' all flustered. I'm not suggesting that, but most young women her age have already begun thinkin' 'bout things like that. And there will be plenty of suitors wherever they settle down, so you might want to prepare yourself for that. Now, if you were to be talkin' to her 'bout such things, she might just set her bonnet for you and not pay any attention to any others, and she would wait for you to get settled and such."

The roadway was lined with overarching tall timber and undergrowth that edged the road, giving the impression of riding through a green tunnel. As they passed, a grey squirrel scolded them, and a bushy-tailed fox crossed the road before them. At the sight of the fox, the dapple-grey mustang sidestepped while the big claybank just nodded his head as he watched the canine scamper into the brush. They moved to one side when a buckboard drawn by a matched pair of bays clattered up the road, undoubtedly bound for the town. A bareheaded farmer type nodded as he slipped forward a mite to shield his little woman who clung to his big arm. Eli nodded back and greeted them with, "Evenin' folks."

"Evenin'," grunted the farmer, looking sidelong at the pair of riders, but did not slow his wagon.

As the dust settled, Eli and Ben were again riding side by side and Eli started to speak when the little grey exploded. The gelding bent in the middle, sidestepped toward Eli as he dropped his head between his front feet and launched himself toward the clouds. Ben grabbed the saddle horn, drove his feet deep in the stirrups and pulled on the reins, trying to pull the horse's head up, but the animal twisted in the air, came down on spring-loaded hooves and sunfished, screaming at the trees as he contorted himself, trying to rid himself of his rider. But Ben held on, his britches glued to the saddle, his one hand trying to milk the saddle horn, the other with the rein wrapped around his wrist and fingers gripping the leather for the worth of his life.

Eli slapped legs to his big claybank and was quickly beside the grey. Reaching for the headstall, he pulled the little mustang's head close, crowding him with the bigger stallion and soon settled the horse down. Eli talked softly to the horse, holding him close and walking both horses a little further on the road. He looked back at a wide-eyed Ben and asked, "What happened?"

"I'm not sure, I think I saw a snake at the edge of the brush, but he blew up 'fore I could tell for sure."

Eli frowned, looking down at the front legs of the grey and told Ben, "Hold him close, I'm gonna look at his legs. See if he got bit or something."

Eli stepped down, ground tied his stallion and moved closer to the grey. After stroking his neck and talking to him to settle him down a little more, he ran his hands down the horse's leg, looking at every part of the legs, searching for any wound or injury, but there was nothing that showed. He stood up, looked at Ben, "I don't see anything. Usually, he wouldn't spook at the sight of a snake, but if it was a rattler, coiled to strike, then yeah. Could you see it? If it was coiled?"

Ben shook his head, reaching down to stroke the neck of the gelding as Eli mounted Rusty. "It was only a glance, I couldn't tell. He," nodding to the horse, "blew up and I grabbed what I could to stay on!"

Eli chuckled, "You did a good job of that!" He reined Rusty around, "Let's head back to the boat. The captain wants to take advantage of what promises to be a clear night with a big moon."

The wood had been loaded and the crew were finishing up the stacks as Eli and Ben returned. They led the horses back aboard, unsaddled them and once in the stalls, they rubbed them down before feeding them some of the grain that Eli had put aboard in St. Louis. He looked at Ben, "They'll be servin' supper soon. You better go to your cabin and see if your ma is ready, she might have you wash up or somethin'."

"As sure as the sun comes up in the mornin', you know she will!" declared Ben, smiling, and laughing. "And after that ride, I could use some freshenin' up!"

———

AFTER SUPPER, as had become common with the cabin passengers, most were taking a stroll around the promenade, taking in the views and the remaining colors of the sunset. Eli was outside his cabin, leaning on the rail, when a woman stopped beside him and asked, "You have the look of a soldier about you, an officer maybe, but no uniform. Were you in the military before?"

Eli stood tall as he turned to look at the woman. He nodded to her, "Ma'am. I'm sorry, I was deep in thought and did not understand what you said." He gave her a quick once-over, noting she was a beautiful woman, maybe early thirties, well dressed and carried herself with dignity and style, yet every bit a lady.

"You have the demeanor of a military man, and I asked if you were in the service before?"

Eli nodded and let a slow smile split his face, "Yes, ma'am. I was in the Union cavalry, served under Sheridan."

"An officer?"

"Yes, ma'am, I held the rank of lieutenant colonel when I was discharged."

"I thought so. You appear to be a man that would be a strong leader and a very effective one I would assume."

"And what has you, a beautiful woman, traveling by yourself in this wild land?" asked Eli. "And what makes you so perceptive regarding the military?"

"Why thank you, Colonel. How very gallant of you." She paused, moved closer to the rail, and looked at the play of light, dim though it was, on the ripples of the water. "I was married to an officer. He was a major in the infantry when he fell. When we lost him, the business of the family fell to me, and I am on my way to Helena."

Eli looked at her, his curiosity rising, but it was not acceptable to be too inquisitive. "I see," he replied.

"No, I'm afraid you don't see. My family has made investments in many things, including railroads and stage lines. We have also invested in some mining ventures, and I prefer to see firsthand what we are investing in…so I travel." She turned to face Eli, "But enough about me, won't your wife be wondering where you are?"

Eli dropped his head and breathed deeply before answering, "My wife is in Heaven."

"Oh, I'm so sorry. I thought the woman at the table with you was your wife."

"No, just a friend. I'm helping her family and the other family at the table get to Helena. Her husband is waiting for her, building a home for her, and they are anxious to be together."

"So, an officer, a leader, and so noble as well. I am impressed!"

Eli grinned, "As am I. It's not every day I meet a beautiful woman that is so self-assured and business savvy. Oh, and my name is Elijah McCain," he stated, nodding, and bowing slightly.

She smiled, extended her hand, and answered, "And I am Constance Wellington."

"Pleased to meet you, Mrs. Wellington."

"Constance."

"Constance it is," answered Eli, smiling broadly as he took her hand in his and bent to kiss the back of her hand. It was a gentlemanly gesture, and the lips barely and lightly touched her hand. She dropped her eyes and did a slight curtsy, smiling just as broadly.

CHAPTER 15

SERVICES

The first light of the rising sun kissed the treetops at the confluence of the Grand and Missouri Rivers. The early rising Eli stood at the rail of the Hurricane deck at the bow of the boat, watching the current nudge the north shore of the big river bend. In moments, the boat was in the morning shadows of the tall trees on the east shore, stretching out to touch the undergrowth on the west shore. It was often easy to see the many changes to the course of the river, the meandering Missouri always sought out the path of least resistance and carried its muddy waters where it willed.

He was stirred from his reverie when a voice asked, "Enjoying the morning, are you?"

Chaplain Haney came to his side and mimicked Eli by leaning on the railing in a similar manner, elbows on the rail, hands clasped together and gaze taking in the pink of the morning bouncing on the ripples of the river.

"I am. I've always enjoyed the quiet of the early

morning as the day begins to reveal itself and push aside the uncertainties of the night."

The pastor turned to look at Eli, a slight frown wrinkling his brow, "That sounds almost poetic."

Eli chuckled, "I'm not much of a poet. It's all I can do to string together enough words to make myself understood."

"You do a fine job of that. But I'm here to ask a favor."

"Shoot."

"We'll have services this morning, and I could use some help moving tables and setting up chairs for the service. I was wondering if I could recruit you?"

Eli chuckled, "The last time I was recruited, it took many years off my life and caused me to duck bullets and arrows from one end of this country to the other!"

"Well, there might be some slinging of hellfire and damnation, but no bullets and arrows," explained the chaplain, smiling.

"Then I'm your man. And I might be able to recruit some help from the breakfast table."

"Thank you, Elijah," replied the chaplain, turning away toward the central salon.

———

THE SALON WAS CROWDED with most of the cabin passengers seated in the many New Haven Folding Chairs, and several of the deck passengers seated on the floor and standing along the walls. The pastor led the people in song with *He Leadeth Me, Angels We Have Heard on High,* and *Jesus Loves Me.*

When the people were seated, the pastor took to the lectern, opening his Bible with an air of reverence and read his text, "From I John 5:13, *These things have I written unto you that believe on the name of the Son of God; that ye may know that ye have eternal life, and that ye may believe on the name of the Son of God.* Now, let us pray." He bent to one knee, put his elbow on his other knee, and held his hand to his forehead and prayed, asking God for His power and for the Spirit to guide his words. As he said, "Amen," he rose and looked at the expectant crowd.

"I know if I was to have those of you that believe that there was a true historical figure by the name of Jesus, raise your hands, probably all of you would do so. But I would like to clarify what I believe is a simple misunderstanding." He paused, moved beside the lectern, resting his arm on the wooden pulpit, and looked at the people, his eyes roving over the crowd as he spoke. "Many believe, that if they just believe there was a Jesus, and maybe even believe that He was the Son of God, that is all they need believe. But I would like to focus our attention on the one of the almost insignificant words in that text, the word *on.*

"You see, it says *believe on the name of the Son of God.* Now, let me explain." He moved away from the lectern and picked up one of the folding chairs and lifted it for everyone to see. "Many of you have never seen these folding chairs before, yet there you are, sitting on them. You're not standing beside an empty chair, but you have rested your entire weight upon them." He sat down to demonstrate. "Now before I sat down, I looked at this chair, and I believed it was a chair, and I even believed it would hold me if I sat in it. But..." he stood, smiling, "Just like right now, all my belief will get me is tired. It's not until I believe *on* the chair, that it does me any good."

He smiled as he looked around the crowd, "And that's the way it is with Jesus. Many of you are like the devils in

James 2:19, *Thou believest there is one God; thou doest well: the devils also believe, and tremble*. You see, it takes more than just believing in the existence of Jesus, it must be that you believe *on*. Just like when I sat in this chair, I believed *on*." He sat in the chair again, crossing his arms on his chest and continued, "See, now I believe on. That means I have put my complete trust in this chair. If it breaks and falls, I fall. But I trust it and I am comfortable." He stood again, motioning to the chair, "So, how do I put my trust in Jesus, you ask? Well, according to Romans 10:9-11, *That if thou shalt confess with thy mouth the Lord Jesus, and shalt believe in thine heart that God hath raised Him from the dead, thou shalt be saved. For the scripture saith, Whosoever believeth on him shall not be ashamed*. And verse 13, *For whosoever shall call upon the name of the Lord shall be saved*."

The chaplain continued, explaining to the people about how to call upon the name of the Lord in prayer and led those who wanted to put their trust in Jesus in a simple prayer. "Dear Lord, I want to put my trust in you and believe on Jesus as my Savior. I ask for forgiveness of my sins and to receive the free gift of salvation so I might be saved. I pray in Jesus' name, Amen."

Many of the people had joined the chaplain as he led the prayer and he looked up, smiling at the crowd and explained about the need to be baptized, "Baptism is the first step of obedience as we tell the world we have been buried in His likeness and rise to a new life in Him. Now, later today, if and when the captain pulls into shore, we'll have a baptism service for all of you that would like to take this step in your new life in Christ."

He closed the service with another hymn, "Lets stand and sing a new song, *Shall We Gather at the River*.

Shall we gather at the river, where bright angel
*   feet have trod,*
With its crystal tide forever, flowing by the throne
*   of God.*
Yes, we'll gather at the river, the beautiful, the
*   beautiful river.*
Gather with the saints at the river, that flows by
*   the throne of God."*

He finished with a prayer of thanksgiving and asking for God's guidance and protection for all present. As the services were dismissed, many made their way to the pastor to comment on the message and shake his hand, but the pastor was watching Eli who stayed seated, his head bowed. When the crowd had dispersed and most of the chairs had been put away, Chaplain Haney sat beside Eli and said, "I noticed you prayed with me and the others to believe on Jesus and accept that gift of eternal life. I'm certain you meant what you prayed, didn't you?"

Eli looked at the pastor, nodded, "Yes. And I thought back on the many times I have questioned God. Because I never heard it explained like you did, I just thought that since I had known about Jesus since I was but a child, that was all it took. But when you said it had to be a personal decision to put all my trust in Him, that struck me to the core. I...well, I can feel the difference, it's like a weight has been lifted off. But, I'm also concerned about my sons, and their mother. She passed some time ago, and I'm not sure about what she believed." He looked at the pastor, the obvious question in his eyes.

Pastor Haney put his hand on Eli's shoulder, "We never know the private communion one has with the Lord, especially in those last moments. But, like you, I was in the war, and I know of several times that men, although they were not what you would call *religious* felt something in those last moments. I believe that God has His angels round about us, and at those times, when someone has the definite desire in his heart to believe *on* the Lord, He makes it possible."

Eli looked down at the floor, slowly shaking his head, "That's comforting, but...it does make me concerned about the boys."

"Well, that my friend, is why you must find them and tell them," explained the pastor.

Eli looked at the pastor, shook his head as he stood, "For now, I've got to go feed my horses!" stated Eli, grinning and shaking the pastor's hand.

CHAPTER 16

LEXINGTON

The forward part of the salon on the Hurricane deck was what some might call the lounge or game room. Several tables were taken by men playing poker, and near the windows of the forward area, several chairs were arranged for the passengers to take in the views or just to have a comfortable sitting area apart from their cabins. Eli was seated in one of the big chairs, holding a newspaper in his hands, yet occasionally glancing around the salon and out the windows, ever vigilant of his surroundings and those about.

He surreptitiously took in the men playing poker and as was his habit, considered each of the men and their manners, trying to determine the nature of their business and way of life. Two of the men he had noticed before and had already determined they were professional gamblers, sometimes working together but always acting as if they were complete strangers. The day before Eli had stood at the rail not too far from them and overheard one of their conversations that revealed they were indeed working together and had been friends or at least acquaintances for some time and had worked the river-boats before. He turned the page of the paper, lifted it high to read a particular article about the number and value of vessels captured by rebel privateers when a soft voice came from behind him.

"Good morning, Colonel. May I join you?"

He quickly lowered the paper and turned to see the very pleasant Constance Wellington. He smiled and replied, "Certainly, Mrs. Wellington," he stood and pulled a chair out and held it for her to be seated.

"Enjoying the morning view, are you?" she asked, smiling.

He chuckled at her jab at his attempt to hide himself from others by burying his face in the newspaper, seemingly oblivious to others and the passing scenery of the river. "I will admit, I have noticed *some* of the scenery. Perhaps it was due to the lack of nearby beauty, but you have resolved that issue by your presence."

"Why, Colonel, how you do go on. And here I thought you to be some isolated recluse that paid little attention to your fellow passengers," she replied, letting a hint of a giggle pass as she turned away to look at the limited scenery on the riverbanks.

"No, not at all. I surmise it is because of so many years in the loneliness of command *and* being away from home and hearth."

Constance nodded and smiled, looking around at the others that were in the salon, some at the game tables, others seated in conversational groups, one man stretched out and his head leaning against the back of the chair, his mouth wide open and his lips fluttering with every snore. She chuckled, "People sometimes make better scenery. Have you ever just looked at others, trying to guess their purpose or history?"

"Yes, ma'am, I think it is a common practice by many that travel among strangers." He looked around at the others and back to Constance, "And what have *you* deduced about those about us?"

She gave the crowd another glance and with a mischievous smile said, "Take the sleeper, for example, I think he is a peddler of sorts, not very successful, but also a lonely man. And the three men at the table, the one with the dark jacket is a money man, maybe a banker, the other two are wannabes that are soaking up all the *wisdom* they believe the banker is privy to, hoping to find some secret to riches." She looked around again, "Those," nodding to the gaming tables, "are two gamblers that think no one knows they are working together and they're doing their best to fleece anyone that is foolish enough to get in the game, like that farmer turned prospector that is sitting between them."

"And what about those three at the table in the corner over there?" suggested Eli, looking at Constance and nodding to the men that leaned into the middle of the table, talking and glancing about.

"Oh, they're the dastardly type. Probably plotting a bank robbery like Jesse James or some stage holdup. The one with his back to us is the ringleader, and he's giving them his foolproof plan. What he doesn't know, is there is no foolproof plan and the evidence of that is usually found hanging from a stout limb of a tall tree!" she declared, grinning a mischievous grin.

Eli smiled, shaking his head, "You have no faith in your fellow man. Not all of these Westerners are brigands." He folded the paper, laid it on the table, and pushed his chair back as he stood. He extended a hand to Constance, "I think we both need some fresh air. Won't you join me for a walk around the promenade?"

Constance smiled, pushed back her chair, accepted his hand, and stood. "After you, my good man."

———

AS THEY WALKED through the tables, Eli saw one table where two couples were playing what he thought was bridge, a game he never had interest in, and two men were busy at another table with cribbage. Other groups were just sitting together, talking and getting acquainted. He thought how this small enclave seemed much like a small town of strangers, a common goal of reaching the end of the line, but most everything—goals, purposes, hopes, and dreams—were different.

As they stepped onto the promenade, the cool air that rose from the river was a refreshing caress on their faces as they looked upriver, seeing the waves push away from the prow of the boat and lap at the shorelines. They walked together in silence, ambling on the deck, passing others that held to the rail or leaned against the posts, many deep in thought, others just passing the time. Constance stopped at the starboard side nearest the prow, glancing back to Eli with a smile, "Do you think we'll stop soon for more wood, or will we make Lexington?"

"Captain says we'll stop just shy of Lexington to take on more wood and some more freight, then since the moon is still big and bright, he hopes to push on past Westport. He's thinkin' about St. Joseph as our next stop."

"Oh, I was hoping we'd stop soon, let us take a meal on shore, take a walk on solid ground," she mused, smiling, and looking at the shoreline. The trees had thinned, and they could see the beginnings of farms and newly constructed homes. A farmer was prodding a team of big plow horses as they leaned into the harness, tilling the soil for the spring planting. She nodded toward the farmer, "It's good to see the new homes, farmland, and more. Our nation is growing, healing from the war, expanding. It's an exciting time, don't you think?"

"It is. Have you been further west before?" he asked, looking down at the expectant and smiling face of Constance.

She dropped her eyes, turned away slightly, and looked to the shore. "My husband and I had a planned trip to Colorado Territory before the war, but..." her shoulders lifted as she sighed at the memory. She lifted her eyes and added, "Most of my travels have been east of the Mississippi. Although I have been to St. Louis before, talked to those with the Pacific Railroad and others. And I made a trip to Jefferson City on the railroad to meet with Ben Holladay of the Overland Express. But..." she lifted her eyes to Eli, "this is my first trip to the northwest."

"Then I think you'll find it somewhat different, less settled, wide-open spaces, and I would like to see your face the first time you see the Rocky Mountains."

"Oh, I've heard about those mountains, and I am anxious to see them." She nodded forward, "But for right now, I think they're calling us to supper. Will you join me?"

"I'd be pleased. Perhaps you can give me more insight into some of our fellow passengers."

———

THE SUN WAS bright upon the waters as they rounded the wide bend and the river turned to the southwest.

Lexington was on the port side, a long sandbar catching the ripples from the boat as it neared the wharf. Eli was on the Texas deck, having taken a folding chair from the salon and was seated forward of the smokestacks. He watched as the wood hawks and crew busied themselves loading the wood, and the roustabouts that were packing some wooden cargo boxes on board to take to the hold. Eli noticed they were marked **Books** and **Bibles** in bold letters, with more printing across the top of the crate. He stood and walked to the side of the deck that was above the gangplank and watched the men carry the cargo boxes, four that he counted, two men to a box. He called down to the men below, "Say, where're those boxes going?"

"I dunno, cain't read!" declared one man, but the other twisted his head around to look straight on and called up, "Says they're goin' to the Blackfoot Mission, care o' Fort Benton!"

Eli lifted his head to acknowledge the man's answer, glanced below to see a man craning around to see who was shouting from above, and pulled back before he could be seen. He did not recognize the man, although he looked familiar. Eli frowned as he turned away and returned to his chair. He was thoughtful as he considered, *Four big shipping containers of Bibles. That's a lot of Bibles, especially for a new mission*. Something was bothering him and then he remembered in the early days of the war and before the war, there were shipments of Bibles to arm the jayhawkers that were actually Sharps rifles. They came to be known as Beecher's Bibles because of Henry Ward Beecher, the ardent antislavery advocate. *But the war's over, and the only people that want rifles in that quantity, are the Natives.*

CHAPTER 17

NIGHTWIND

Eli stood in the pilothouse with the captain who was busy at the wheel. The moon was high overhead and the moonbeams bounced off the waves as the boat pushed its way against the current. Even though the chugging of the steam engine driving the long shafts that turned the stern paddle wheel was a relentless sound, Eli had become so accustomed to the rhythm it was as if the boat traveled in silence. The only recognizable sound was that of waves slapping against the hull and the churning of the water at the stern paddle wheel. The boat rounded the sharp bend back to the north as the current from the confluence with the Kansas River pushed against the port side of the boat. With deep water assured, the captain kept the course, seldom checking the magnetic compass mounted on the post of the wheel.

Eli asked, "Isn't it difficult to see any floating debris that might damage the boat?"

The captain chuckled, nodding forward, "That's what those three lookouts are for, with the long poles, they push aside anything that might be a threat. The one at the bow sounds the alarm, and if it looks to be too big a hazard, he'll shout up to me." He glanced to Eli and back to the river, "Usually, I can see anything that's big enough for concern before they do and make any necessary moves. Hereabouts, with deep water, the only threat might be some big, uprooted sweepers but we can usually spot them before there's any danger."

After the confluence with the Kansas, the Missouri pointed to the north then made a wide bend to the west. After a few more bends to the north and again to the west, the Big Muddy took a northerly course, the moon climbing higher off their right shoulder. They had pushed past Independence, Westport, Kansas City, and were now bound for St. Joseph. Eli looked at the captain, "Think we'll make St. Joseph 'fore the sun sets again?"

The captain grinned, "Maybe, but when you've been on the water as much as I have, you learn to focus on the present time and place and let the morrow's problems take care of themselves." He nodded to the heavy clouds that hid the stars in the northern sky, "Like those clouds there, they'll probably let loose of all that water they're carrying and slow us down a mite. It's difficult to see the sandbars, snags, sweeps, and such, when the rain is pelting the river, so we have to either slow down or tie up till it passes. But, this stretch of the river is usually deep enough to keep travelin', as long as we keep a watch out."

Eli tried to appear casual as he looked at the river and the clouds then leaned back against the side of the pilot-house, looking at the captain. "Say, I noticed the roustabouts takin' on some freight at Lexington, appeared to be boxes of books and Bibles. I didn't know there was any mission up there near Fort Benton."

"I don't think there is, but you know these 'men of the cloth' and what we call foolishness they call faith. I guess they, whoever *they* are, think they'll need to give a lot of Bibles out to Natives that can't read in order to build their mission."

"Will you be takin' on any more freight?"

"Nope. We're loaded now. No room for another box or another passenger. The only stops we'll be makin' will be for wood."

The captain leaned forward, looking up at the dark clouds, "And here it comes!" As if waiting for the cue from the captain, the storm clouds pulled the plug on their tankards of water and let it loose. The downpour pelted the pilothouse. Driven by a strong wind, the rain slapped at the big boat, totally obscuring the view of the river. The captain shouted to be heard above the thunderous rain assaulting the pilothouse, "Slide open those windows!" nodding to the forward windows.

Eli frowned, "But, the rain..." he motioned, taking a step forward.

"Open 'em, I can't see through the glass!" shouted the captain.

Eli quickly slid the windows aside, opening the pilothouse to the brunt of the storm. The rain splattered about, and within moments, everything in the pilothouse was drenched. The captain had kicked the doors of the map cabinet that stood behind the wheel, closed. With one hand on the wheel, the captain grabbed for the bell pulls to the engine room, giving it a pull to sound the signal to reduce speed. In just a moment, the pitman shafts slowed, and the paddle wheel reduced its churning. But the boat still chugged away, driving against the current of the Big Muddy, moving headfirst into the wind-driven deluge. The roar of the wind, the pelting of the rain, and the chug of the engines hampered the communication from the prow watchers and the pilothouse.

The captain glanced to Eli, nodding to the prow, "Could you go to the forward edge of the deck, watch the prow, and relay any warning?"

Eli nodded, turned to the door, and quickly went to the forward edge of the Texas deck beyond the smoke-stacks. He dropped to his haunches, pulled his hat down tight, shading his face and eyes from the torrential down-pour, to watch the three men at the prow. They were on their knees, looking at the water of the river, staring into the darkness and downpour, watching for sweepers and snags as well as ensuring the boat stayed in the deep-water current. The foremost watcher shouted, pointing before them, and turned back to look at the pilothouse. He cupped his hands and shouted, "Bear to starboard! Bear to starboard! Sandbar on port side!"

Eli turned back to face the pilothouse, mimicking the forward watcher and repeated his order exactly. The captain answered with a "Yo!" and Eli thought he felt the boat move to the starboard. Little did he know that an experienced pilot or captain often steered the boat by feel, knowing the way the boat moved in the current and when the current pushed the bow to one side or the other. The captain and crew knowingly referred to the boat as 'she' or 'her,' but it wasn't just because of the tradition, it was more the way the boat responded to the slightest touch by the pilot and the crew.

The storm had awakened the pilot, Barnaby Nichols, and he reported to the pilothouse. Aiding the captain as an additional lookout, the experience and knowledge of both men regarding the Big Muddy, lent itself well to the journey in the midst of the torrent. Although it had been little more than an hour of raging storm before it began to abate, it seemed like an eternity to those that fought the forces of nature. But when the deluge subsided to a mild rainfall, and the moon slid from behind the dark clouds, the crew resembled drowned rats and as they were relieved, headed to their quarters. Eli stuck his head in the pilothouse, "If you don't need me anymore, I'm goin' to my cabin!"

The captain chuckled, "Thanks, Eli, you were a big help. Couldn't have done it without you!" He stepped away from the wheel, allowing the pilot to take over, "And I'm goin' to my bunk too!" The open windows had allowed the almost horizontal rain to drench the captain who never wavered in his duty at the helm. "How 'bout we meet at the salon for a hot breakfast and a pot of hot coffee?" he asked, as he joined Eli. The men were headed for the stairway to the Hurricane, or Cabin deck and Eli nodded, chuckling, "Now that sounds good. I'll see you there!"

————

THE SLOW-RISING sun that stretched shadows toward the west, found Eli at a table in the salon as the galley crew busied themselves with the making of breakfast. He had his newspaper and opened it before him, searching the pages for any article he had yet to peruse and focused on a reprint of an article from the Salt Lake *Vidette* that announced the assassination of another resident of Utah by Brigham Young's miscreants. As he read the article, he frowned at the explanation of the man named Brassfield who became enamored with the second wife of a Mormon by the name of Hill and married her. But when he went to get her belongings, he was arrested and later was murdered by a shot to the back during the trial. He shook his head and turned the page just as a familiar voice asked, "Are you alone?"

He turned to see the smiling Constance and he quickly stood, pulling out the chair beside him, motioning for her to be seated, "Yes, I am alone. Won't you join me?"

As she was seated, Eli explained, "I think the captain may soon join us and I was thinking about asking him about the verity of your observations of our fellow passengers," he smiled as he folded the paper and put it on the chair beside his hip.

"That just might be interesting. Are you willing to place a wager on my deductions? Say, one dime for every correct answer, payable to me, and the same to you for every incorrect answer?"

Eli chuckled, "I dunno, that might get awful expensive. Don't know if I can afford it, of course, if I win out, can you afford it?"

"Afford what?" asked the captain as he pulled out a chair opposite the two bettors.

Eli chuckled and explained to the captain, "So, if we ask you about a particular passenger, you'll know there's money on the line."

"Do I get a cut?"

"How many ways can you cut a dime?" asked Constance, laughing at the men.

As the passengers filed in and took their places at the tables, one man and a couple joined them at their table. As they seated themselves, Constance smiled, looked at Eli and with one eyebrow lifted, she waited until the captain introduced the newcomers. Captain Marsh began the introductions with a nod to the couple, "Folks, this is Elijah McCain and Constance Wellington," with a motion of his hand, "And this fine couple is Martine Beaumont and his wife, Amélie. They are going to set up a mercantile store in Helena. And this is Gunther Becker, he will be putting in a bakery, also in Helena."

The men extended hands to shake with Eli, nodding to Constance, as Martine asked, "And now that you know what we will be doing, what is it that you do, Mr. McCain?"

"Well, for the past almost twenty years, I've been a military man. But now, I'm, well, I guess you could say an explorer. I'm exploring just what it is that I will do," answered Eli.

"And you?" he asked, as he turned his face toward Constance.

"My company is in investments. We'll be looking at some properties in Helena and Virginia City and..." she shrugged, holding one hand up, palm up. She looked to Eli with a smile and a nod to Mr. Becker, who she thought was a banker, and slipped Eli his first dime.

CHAPTER 18

NORTHBOUND

They were two weeks out of St. Louis when the boat nosed into the levee on the west side. The sun was bright in their faces as the crew threw the ropes to the men on the wharf. Eli stood, lead ropes of Rusty and the dapple grey in hand, anxious to be on solid ground. The captain said they would overnight here, with cargo to offload and wood to procure, it would be midmorning before they took to the river again. Eli needed to get the kinks out, not just his but his horses as well. It had been four days of riding in the stalls and the horses would relish some fresh grass and a chance to stretch out, as would Eli.

As soon as the gangplank touched ground, Eli led the horses down to the long sloping shore, mounted up and turned his back to the boat and his face to the trees. Rusty was stretching his legs, prancing a mite, and turned back to look at Eli as if to say, "Well?" Eli chuckled, understanding his big stallion and slapped legs to the big horse. Rusty lunged forward, almost jerking Eli from the saddle as they hit the length of the lead rope for the grey, but his tight grip jerked the grey to stretch out as well and within moments, the buildings of Nebraska City were behind them and obscured by the trees and long shadows of coming dusk.

Eli pulled his big horse back to a trot and then to a walk. He reached down to stroke the dun's neck, talking to him and pulled the grey alongside for some of the same attention. He sat up when he heard the clatter of hooves of running horses coming from a side road and watched the trees as two riders came into the main road. They quickly reined up when they saw Eli, and with a bit of scowl, one growled, "What're you doin' here?" Both men were jerking at the reins of the horses, the animals were skittish and appeared fearful of the riders.

The speaker was a lantern-jawed ruffian-looking type, somewhat scruffy with about a two- or three-day growth of whiskers, hair that covered his dirty collar, and a belly that hid his belt. He appeared to be a good six feet tall and probably well over two hundred pounds with an attitude of about the same size. His coat was a grey uniform great coat that showed the faded evidence of a couple of stripes. A quick glance showed both men wore parts of Confederate uniforms. The second man was obviously the hanger-on, the type that fed the ego of the bully of the two. A little smaller but just as unkempt as his partner and he laughed with a snort and a snicker at each remark made by his partner.

Eli looked at the two but did not respond. The big man spoke again, "I axt you a question!" as he glanced back down the road they came from and back at Eli.

Eli looked from one to the other, glanced down as he wrapped the lead line of the grey around the saddle horn and looked back up at the two. "Didn't figger it was any of your business!"

The talker snarled, gigged his horse forward to crowd closer to Eli and growled, "I'm makin' it my bizness! Now answer me!" He nodded to his partner who also came closer. The big man looked at Eli's horses, especially the big red dun stallion, "An' I might make that horse muh bizness too!"

Eli casually leaned his right elbow on the saddle horn, which put his hand near the butt of his pistol that was out of sight under the edge of his jacket, and with a shrug, slipped his left hand behind his back, as if he had to scratch an itch. Eli grinned, "Well now, just cuz you say it's your business, doesn't make it so. Sometimes when folks get too nosy or thinkin' they can take whatever they want, they end up gettin' hurt and wishin' they'd minded their own business."

He grinned as he appeared casual, leaning forward, looking at the men. The big man growled, threw back the tail of his jacket as he grabbed for his pistol that sat high on his hip. He glanced up just in time to see two pistols in the hands of Eli, one pointed at him and the other at his partner. The cocking of the hammers sounded loud in the narrows between the trees and both men sucked wind as their eyes flared and they leaned back, slowly lifting their hands as the big man stuttered, "Uh...uh... we was just curious, mister. Didn't mean nothin'."

Before Eli could say anything, the sound of another horse coming at a good clip and up the same road got his attention. A big plow horse with a woman aboard came lumbering from the road and slid to a stop beside the others. The woman had a rifle laying across the withers of the big horse that she was riding bareback and astraddle. She grabbed at the rifle and barked, "You another'n?"

"Whoa up there, woman! Can't you see I'm holding

these men? What happened that's got you so riled?" asked Eli, frowning at the rifle-wielding woman, who even with the windblown hair and her dress bunched up around her legs, showed herself to be a pretty good-looking woman. He let a slow grin split his face and asked, "Well?"

"They stole our horses! I didn't see 'em till they came from the barn and 'fore I could get to my rifle, they were gone!" answered the woman, her chest heaving with the exertion of staying atop and handling the plow horse and her rifle at the same time.

Eli grinned, nodded, and looked at the men, "So, horse thieves huh?"

Both men dropped their eyes, mumbling to themselves, but kept their hands high. Eli looked at the woman, "You wanna come into town with me to turn these two over to the sheriff?"

"Won't do no good. Town don't have a sheriff, just a deputy and it's not too often you can find him when he's sober."

"So, what do you want me to do with 'em, shoot 'em?"

The woman looked at Eli, eyes wide, and glanced at the two thieves. "Tempting, but maybe not. Best try to find the deputy and let him and the good townsfolk deal with 'em."

"Then you might need to come into town with me to tell the deputy what happened." Eli looked from the woman to the men, "You two," motioning to the men, "get down." He looked back at the woman, "Ma'am, if you'll step down and send that horse home, you might ride one of these," motioning to the other two horses, "and send the other'n home too. Those two," motioning to the outlaws, "can walk."

"Walk!?" whined the second man, looking from Eli to his partner.

"Ummhmm," answered Eli, watching the woman slide to the ground and throw the rein over the neck of her horse and face him down the road. With a slap on his rump, the big plow horse started back to the farm. She did the same with one of the two stolen horses and swung aboard the second. But with the saddle on, she was able to hook one knee over the pommel and ride the saddle a little more sedately.

Eli stepped to the ground, handed his Colt to the woman, "Keep 'em covered while I secure them a mite."

He used a long piece of twine he kept in his saddle-bags and soon had the men's hands tied behind them and used as additional length to tie their elbows together, making them walk close beside one another and hindering their ability to run off. The men grumbled all the while, but Eli just chuckled and soon mounted up, holstered his pistol, and nudged the men forward with the chest of his big stallion.

Town was a little less than two miles and by the time they rode into town, following the two bound prisoners, Eli had learned that Adelaide Chatham was a war widow and lived alone with her mother, struggling to keep the farm going, and with two youngsters—boys, aged nine and eleven—helping out. She had been a widow going on five years and the neighbor farmer had been doing his best to court her, although she was somewhat hesitant to be much more than neighbors and friends. "He's really quite helpful, but...well, I just don't see him as a husband type. For that matter, no other woman seems to, either, except maybe Cordelia. She has the hotel in town, middle-aged, never married, and lonely," she smiled and stifled a giggle as she explained.

"Well, Adelaide, I haven't had supper yet, so, how about after we drop these two off at the jail, you join me for supper?"

Adelaide dropped her eyes, smiling, and looked up and said, "I'd like that. It's been some time since I've had dinner without the boys under foot."

———

THE SUN HAD long bid adieu and the western sky was losing its colors when Eli led the horses up the gangplank and into the boat. He put them away, gave them both a good rubdown, and climbed the steps to the cabin deck. Harriet Hamilton and Constance Wellington were standing at the rail, talking with one another, when Eli's feet hit the deck. Constance was facing the steps and was the first to see him and gave a slight smile and wave, as she listened to Harriet talking about her children.

Eli nodded, tipped his hat, and went into the salon, choosing a table near a wall-mounted lantern. He had a hot off the presses copy of the *Nebraska City News* newspaper under his arm that he received from editor, J. Sterling Morton, who he met when he and Adelaide were dining in the hotel dining room. After talking with Morton about the more recent happenings, he was anxious to get a few more details from the newspaper. They had talked about some common acquaintances, a Major General Grenville Dodge and a Colonel Patrick O'Connor who had been instrumental and involved in the failed Powder River Expedition against the Lakota, Cheyenne, and Arapaho. Morton had said, "Since that debacle, the Sioux under a chief name of Red Cloud, have been somewhat cantankerous. They're supposed to be trying to make another treaty, but I'm thinkin' ol'

Red Cloud is gonna be too smart for them soldier boys."

"Has anything in particular been happening that you know about?" asked Eli, concerned about the boat going into Cheyenne, Crow, and Sioux territory. He had been in a few scrapes with both the Sioux and Cheyenne while he was at Fort Laramie and had considerable respect for the Natives and their ability to wage war.

"Only that Red Cloud and some of his Oglala were headin' for Fort Laramie, willing to talk about treaty. But there's been so many gold hunters that have taken the Bozeman Trail up to the Montana gold country, there have been some conflicts, leaving both white men and Indians dead. I'm thinkin' Red Cloud doesn't want the Bozeman Trail through their territory, which was supposed to be given to them exclusively by the last Fort Laramie treaty," expounded the newspaperman.

"I know, I was there about that time, and if I remember correctly, it goes right through the land of the Sioux and the land of the Crow." Eli shook his head, remembering his time at Fort Laramie, and the many times he met with the leaders of the Sioux, the Crow, and others. He knew the Natives and their reverence for the land of their people, and he also knew the white men and their utter disregard for the land and the Native people. He had long known this disparity of cultures and lifestyles was a perfect formula for war in the West and he had enough of war.

Chapter 19

Challenges

"I thought you didn't have any room for more freight, and now I see ten Herefords down below!" stated Eli, looking across the table at the captain.

The captain chuckled, "When I told you that, we were loaded full. But after offloading all the freight for Russell, Majors, and Waddell to take across country to the new forts out west, well..." he shrugged as he accepted his plate of breakfast from the server.

"I thought they were more into stagecoaches, not freight," queried Eli, lifting a steaming cup of coffee.

"They are, but they got their start with freight. Nebraska City was their main port for shipping goods west."

"And the cattle?"

"To the end of the line. Miners get hungry for beefsteak and are willing to pay a premium for it. I heard of one place last fall that charged thirty dollars for one steak!"

Eli frowned, shaking his head, "A fool and his money..." and took a long draft of hot coffee.

The captain nodded to the folded paper beside Eli and asked, "Anything new in the paper?"

Eli sat the coffee cup down and leaned forward, his forearms on the edge of the table. "Only that Red Cloud and the Sioux are making war talk. And we're going right through the middle of their land."

The captain frowned, reaching for his coffee. He looked at Eli, "So, you're thinkin' we might be gettin' a visit from some of his people?"

"Not for a while yet, but yeah. At least it wouldn't surprise me. When the young bucks get to lookin' for scalps, honors, blood, captives, they'll do just about anything. Trouble is, most of the older men don't have much say in the matter. The Natives are different from whites. You see, among the whites, there's kind of an authority. Whenever somebody in authority says that's the way things are, then that's the way it is. But with the Natives, their chiefs just advise, counsel, lead, but never just dictate. That's different than what we're used to, especially in the military. If a leader—officer if you will—says do or don't do something, then that's the way it is. But the Natives, and I've seen this among many different tribes, they don't believe anyone has the right to tell you what to do, it's up to you to decide for your own self.

"Now, if there's a good leader, and he says, let's go on a raid, then any young buck that wants to go, well, he'll up and go. And if he's an especially good leader, then most of the warriors will choose to follow him. But if one or two or so say nope, then they'll stay home, no repercussions.

"That's why it's difficult to make treaties. The ones that sign, yeah, they give their words to do as agreed. But all those that don't sign, well, they just do whatever they want."

The captain leaned back, looking at Eli somewhat skeptically, "Then why have chiefs?"

"Some inherit it from their fathers, others earn the right to sit in council and advise the others. Now the council, they can make major decisions and the others are expected to follow, and if some young buck goes against their ways, traditions, or tribal laws, then they'll get banished and are forced from the village. But that's rare."

The captain finished his breakfast, had his coffee topped off, and with cup in hand, he rose from the table, and looked at Eli, "Say, next time you go ashore on those horses, if you see a deer or something else, how 'bout bringing it back. We could use some fresh meat."

"Just bring it back? Don't you want me to shoot it first?"

The captain chuckled, "Well, if you think you can rope a deer or a buffalo and drag it back alive, you go right ahead. We could use some entertainment."

Eli chuckled, "I'll see what I can do, Captain."

———

FIVE DAYS out of Nebraska City, their stop at Sioux City brought fresh water, a full load of firewood, and no significant news. The Big Muddy turned to the west as they put Sioux City behind them, and Eli joined the captain in the pilothouse. "The river looks to be a mite lower than before," suggested Eli, showing a slight frown as he shaded his eyes. The sun was behind them, and the long shadows stretched along the riverbanks. The meandering river was often deceptive to all but the experienced eye of the river pilots and masters.

"It'll get lower. We passed the confluence with the

Little Sioux River 'fore we hit Sioux City, and that," nodding to the north bank, "is the Big Sioux River. Soon we'll be passing the confluence with the Vermillion and the James, and after those, it drops considerably. That's when the channel gets a little sketchy and we have to watch for sandbars, snags, and such. Especially at this time of year, when the spring snowmelt comes from the mountains, and early spring rains wash away riverbanks and bring trees and such downstream."

"In about four days, we'll make Yancton, after we pass the Vermillion and the James." He nodded off his right shoulder, "All that north of the river, that's Dakota Territory."

———————

THE SUN WAS high overhead when they passed the fledgling settlement of Vermillion. The river was wide and the navigable channel narrow, wide sandbars on the south side threatened to encroach into the channel, when Eli said, "Whoa up!" and pointed to the south bank that was suddenly a moving mass of dark brown. The captain grabbed for the bell rope and sounded the code to stop and reverse the engines. The big boat slowed, the current pushing against the shallow hull, and when the big paddle wheel creaked and groaned and began churning the water, white foam sloshed and splashed, and the awkward riverboat stilled and slowly began to backwater.

The massive herd of bison charged across the sandbars, splashed into the water, and bobbed across the current, oblivious to the big boat that slowly retreated. Eli had gone to the point of the Texas deck, watching the massive herd that seemed endless as it stretched to the south of the river. *Must be thousands!* He looked around, heard excited voices from the cabin deck, all talking and pointing and marveling at the rare sight of the massive herd of beasts.

Eli felt the big boat moving, sideslipping toward the north bank. He looked back at the pilothouse and returned to see if he could be of any help. The captain spoke, "I'm gonna tie up over yonder," nodding to some towering cottonwoods. "It looks like it'll take a while for that herd to cross, and we need to steer clear. 'Sides, it'll give the passengers time for a good look and a sight they'll probably never see again."

"Can I be of any help?" asked Eli.

"We've got it in hand. I already sent the mate below; he'll direct the crew and we'll be tied off in a jiffy."

Eli nodded and went below to the cabin deck, walked the promenade until he saw Constance and Harriet and stopped beside them. The ladies turned and Constance said, "Well, you've been keeping yourself scarce lately. Been busy?"

"No, not especially. Not since I went into Nebraska City. Just the usual, taking care of the horses, enjoying the scenery." He nodded to the herd, "Ever seen the like?"

"Never! Isn't it marvelous?" asked Constance, leaning against the rail as if she could get a little closer and see a little more.

Harriet smiled and said, "It's a wonder how the calves can keep up with their mothers!" she nodded at a pair of orange calves swimming beside their mothers and struggling to keep their heads above water.

Eli asked, "Have you had buffalo steak before?"

Both ladies shook their heads and Harriet asked, "Is it tasty?"

"Very. Maybe I oughta get Ben and take him with me to get some fresh meat."

"I don't know right where he is, but if you find Maribel, you'll find him," answered Harriet, smiling.

———

THEY WERE IN THE TREES, near the edge of the passing herd. The movement of the animals had slowed, the leaders stopping for graze and the herd spreading out in the open park that lay behind the line of trees near the river. Eli handed the big Spencer to Ben, whose big eyes lit up and his face split in a smile. He looked at Eli, "Really?"

Eli smiled, nodding, "Think you can do it?"

"I can sure try."

"Alright, down on one knee...now put your elbow on the other...and pick your target."

Ben did as directed, the rifle to his shoulder as he said, "That cow there, by itself. Like you said, it doesn't have a calf."

"Good, now bring the hammer to a full cock, take your sight, and when you're ready, squeeze off your shot."

Eli stood beside him, using a tree for a rest as he lifted his Winchester. He watched Ben, saw him take a breath and let a little out and slowly squeeze the trigger. The big Spencer boomed, bucked, and rocked the young man back, but Ben was stalwart and held his ground, looking at the cow. The animals nearby flinched but did not spook and the targeted cow took a step, staggered, stumbled, and fell. "I got it!" declared Ben, excited as he looked up at Eli.

Eli grinned, "You sure did! Good shootin'! But now, the work begins. Let's get the horses and get started."

"I'll get 'em!" declared an excited Ben, handing the Spencer to Eli as he started into the trees as fast as he could go. Eli chuckled as he watched the young man, remembering the first time he had taken a bison so many years ago as a young lieutenant at Fort Laramie.

As they neared the carcass, the herd moved away but continued their lazy grazing. The horses were more skittish than the bison, but Eli calmed them down and quickly started the field dressing of the big cow. He handed off the knife to Ben and gave all advice needed as the enthusiastic young man split the big beast from gullet to stern and bloodied himself as he dug into the carcass to drag out the innards. The steam rose and the smell permeated the area, causing the herd to move away from the smell of death. Carrion eaters were gathering, buzzards and ravens circling overhead, and some getting anxious for their share as they made quick forays to the gut pile for scraps and scurried away, entrails dragging behind.

"We'll just gut it and drag the rest back to the boat," explained Eli as he went to his horse and retrieved a braided riata. He wrapped the loop around the neck of the beast, mounted up and with the riata wrapped around the saddle horn, dug heels to the big stallion, and said, "Let's go, boy, we need to get this beast back to the boat." The claybank stallion dug in his hooves and leaned into the task, pulling on the heavy load. Once they got moving, the stallion kept going, always digging in, and soon was at the riverbank where the gangplank awaited. Eli kept moving, pointed the stallion to the gangplank and started up, hooves digging and slipping, and Eli reined up, reached down to pat the horse on his neck, and said, "That's good enough, boy, hold steady." Eli loosed the riata from the saddle horn, tossed it back toward the carcass and continued onto the boat. He waved to Ben to bring the grey aboard, and turned to the Mate, "You wanna pull that aboard, or do you think we oughta cut it up a little."

The mate looked at him with a blank stare, shook his head, and walked away. He called over his shoulder, "You shot it, you take care of it!"

CHAPTER 20

LAKOTA

"Say! Ain'tchu...? grumbled the whiskery faced, buckskin clad, bowlegged man that had just come aboard. He had mounted the steps to take a look back from the promenade walk as the boat pulled away from the wharf at Yancton, Dakota Territory. The mountain man looking scruff of a man with a floppy out-of-shape hat that appeared to be growing from his topknot, scowled at Eli, his mind working at remembering where he knew this man from until the big man let a slow grin split his face as he stepped closer, "Twofer! I never 'spected to see you still walkin' on those bowlegs! You're 'sposed to be long dead and stinkin'! Now, you got the stinkin' part down, but near as I can tell, you ain't dead!" declared Eli, reaching out his hand to shake with the mountain man, who slapped his hand aside and caught the bigger man in a bear hug.

The old man looked up at Eli, "Last I heerd o' you, you'ns was 'posed to be goin' off to war an' whip them rascals to a frazzle! I figgered you'd go git yoresef' kilt, whatfer you was wearin' that purty blue unnyform an' makin' yoresef' a good target. But I 'spose them what was shootin' atchu couldn't hit the side of a barn iffn' they was standin' inside it! Lucky fer you!"

Both men chuckled and Eli said, "Let's go in yonder and get us some coffee and talk a spell."

As the two longtime friends seated themselves at the table and the server poured their coffee, Eli looked at Twofer, shook his head and asked, "You know, Twofer, I always meant to ask, where'd you get a handle like Twofer?"

The old man cackled showing his two remaining teeth and explained, "It were at the last ronnyvous, back in '33 I think it were, we'ns was havin' a hawk throwin' contest and them youngsters din't know what they was a doin', so I said, 'Hyar, watch this. I'll make a twofer!' an' I took a hawk in each hand, threw 'em at the target together an' buried 'em both in the stump. Them fellers was so amazed, they forgot muh real name an' called me Twofer e'er since!"

Eli shook his head, amazed, "That was over thirty years ago! Say, just how old are you?"

"Old 'nuff to know better, young 'nuff to do it anyway!" He cackled some more, shook his head, and took a long drink of coffee. As he sat the cup down, he said, "Don' rightly know how old I is, don't really care neither!"

"So, you headin' to the goldfields?"

"Dunno," he mumbled, looking around at the others in the salon. Since it was not mealtime, the only ones at the tables were either involved in card games or visiting, none paying any attention to the two friends. Twofer looked at Eli, "I spent the winter with the Brulé Lakota, Spotted Tail's camp. His daughter *Ah-ho-appa*, Spotted Leaf, took care o' me all winter an' she talked a lot. Tol' me that Red Cloud's Oglala, they be fixin' to make war. She only tol' me cuz Spotted Tail don't like what Red Cloud's doin'. He don' want no war. After what happened at Grattan's Massacre, he done got it figgered it don't do no good to fight the white man, they's too powerful to his way o' thinkin', so he's wantin' peace."

Eli frowned, "I thought Red Cloud was on his way to Fort Laramie to talk peace?"

"He was, an'll prob'ly talk with 'em. But Leaf tol' me his people're 'spectin' to get some good rifles from some'eres. They figger that's the onliest thing keepin' 'em from defeatin' the sol'jer boys. Wit' rifles like the white man, they'd make fearsome fightin' men, that's fer dang shore."

"Did they say when or where they're gonna be getting these rifles?"

"Nary a word. Jes' said they's gettin' some, bunches o' rifles an' ammynition too!"

Eli sat back, frowning as he lifted his coffee cup and took a long sip. He cocked one eyebrow up, squinted at the mountain man, and said, "I might know somethin' about that."

Twofer frowned, leaned closer and asked, "What'chu mean?"

Eli glanced around, saw several others at the tables and leaned back, laughed, and spoke quietly to the older man, "Drink your coffee, meet me at the rail at the front of the boat." He nodded, stood, and pushed the chair back, shook hands as if they were parting, and turned away to go to the promenade walk. Twofer bided his time, sipped his coffee as he made a quick look around the salon and as he sat down the empty cup, he stretched, yawned, and stood to leave. As he turned toward the door at the side of the salon, his casual survey of the people noted a group of four men that seemed to be conferring quietly with one another, no coffee, no drinks, and no cards. None looked especially prosperous, save one whose back was to the mountain man, and he also seemed to be the leader as the others paid close attention to what he was saying.

As Twofer approached Eli, he was motioned to go to the upper deck, also known as the Texas deck, where few passengers would go, but the crew's quarters were below the pilothouse, and they often crowded the stairs to-and-fro to their duties. The two men mounted the steps and went forward, standing at the rail and watching the river. They were alone and could speak freely as Eli began to explain about the cargo boxes marked 'Bibles and Books' that he suspicioned were rifles and ammunition. "It's a trick used by Henry Beecher when he was arming the antislavery crowd in Kansas. They got to calling the Sharps rifles, Beecher's Bibles. I saw 'em load four boxes, but I don't know what else is down there, in the hold, I mean." Eli considered what Twofer had said about the Sioux expecting rifles, frowned and looked at Twofer, "You said Red Cloud's people were expecting rifles, but we won't be in Sioux country until we reach the White River, that's still a couple hundred miles. And the boxes are addressed to a mission somewhere near Fort Benton, but if the shipment goes to Fort Benton, that's nowhere near Sioux country, that's Crow and Blackfeet, even Assiniboine."

"Ummhmm, but from the Heart River to the Yellerstone, that there's Gros Ventre and Arikara, both o' 'em friendly with the Sioux."

"I think we need to talk to the captain, see if we can check those boxes to be sure if they're rifles, and then..." he shrugged as he turned back to look at the river. After a moment, he said, "Let's meet for supper and I'll talk to the captain, maybe have him join us for supper."

"I'se allus one to eat! But, I don' have no cabin. Us po' folks hafta make do wit' whatever we got or kin ketch."

"You join us, I'll buy."

"Hehehe, I'll fer certain do that!" declared the grinning mountain man.

———

"ELI, Twofer, this is my Mate, Hunter Fleming. Hunter, this is Elijah McCain, formerly Colonel McCain of the Union cavalry under General Sheridan, and this is Twofer, his friend." The captain motioned to each man as he introduced them around the table. He had chosen what was sometimes referred to as the captain's table, a smaller table than most and situated in the corner near the bow and stairs allowing for quick access to the pilot-house, if needed. The men were seated, and the servers brought their platters of food which the men passed as they took their portions. As the meal progressed, the captain asked Eli, "Well, you said you had something special to talk about, so..." and motioned with a wave of his hand to the others.

Eli was a little skeptical of the mate but had to trust the captain's judgment and began to detail the discussion regarding the Sioux and the possibility of having a cargo of rifles aboard. "So, Captain, I have a couple questions for you. I noticed the cargo boxes in question were addressed to the Blackfoot Mission, care of Fort Benton. But, if someone was to ask for those boxes before we get to Fort Benton, you know, providing all the necessary papers an' such, would you offload them before Fort Benton?"

"If, as you say, they have the necessary papers, I would be obligated to surrender that cargo to whoever has the papers."

"Is there any other time that those boxes might be taken off the boat, not by someone with papers, but for any other reason?"

"The only time we shift cargo is when we have low water or other hindrance. For example, if a sandbar requires us to 'grasshopper' over, we sometimes offload cargo to get across the sandbar, but without wagons and such, that's rare. Although at the Dauphin Rapids, there are usually wagons and such, because boats often have to lighten the load to make it past the rapids. Sometimes that cargo is taken overland by the wagons, sometimes just up past the rapids and reloaded."

"And where are the Dauphin Rapids?"

"About a hundred twenty miles below Fort Benton."

"Could we look at those boxes, just to be sure about the contents? If it is Bibles and books, then this conversation is moot," offered Eli.

"I cannot allow you to have access to the cargo, but if I don't know about it..." he shrugged. "However, my mate will be glad to give you a tour of the boat at your convenience, just so you know your way around."

The captain rose, excused himself, and headed for the stairs to the Texas deck. The mate, ever the stoic man, looked at Eli and glanced to Twofer, "When you want this tour?"

"When would it be convenient for you?" asked Eli.

"Fewer folks about after dark. I'll meet you for'd by the hold after it's good'n dark," stated the mate, rising and leaving without so much as a glance or another word.

Eli looked at Twofer, motioned to the server for more coffee and once served, turned to Twofer. "You with me on this?"

"Wun't miss it fer nuthin'! Need some excitement in muh ol' age."

CHAPTER 21

DISCOVERY

The handheld brass ship's lantern cast a small arc of light in the damp blackness of the hold. With an interior height of less than four feet, Eli and Twofer crawled on hands and knees, pushing aside heavy cargo containers as they moved toward the stern of the boat. "There! Whassat?" asked Twofer, pointing to boxes pushed to the rear.

Eli lifted the lantern, squinting in the dim light and crawled and scooched closer. With the lantern held as high as the space allowed, he answered, "This is them! Hand me that crowbar."

They swapped, Twofer holding the lantern as Eli manipulated the crowbar. With a heave ho, he pried open the lid of the box, the nails squealing in protest. He paused, listening, but with no movement overhead, he continued and had the corner of the box open. By the dim light, he rummaged through the packed books and Bibles, quickly recognizing the books made nothing more than a layer of packing. He stacked the books beside the box and felt around, grinned and nodding as he extracted a greasy Sharps rifle. "Reckon there's at least eighteen, twenty rifles. Ammunition boxes between the rifles but could be more." He sat back on his haunches, looking at the rifle that lay alongside the box. Craning around to see more, he counted at least six boxes. He frowned, "That means they loaded more before. That means they've got over a hundred rifles here. And these are carbines which use the paper cartridges and that would make them easy to use by the mounted Natives."

"So, what'chu gonna do?"

"Dunno, but we can't let these get into the hands of the Sioux, or any other tribe. The young bucks would think they were invincible with weapons like these."

Eli replaced the rifle and ammunition box, resealed the cargo box and the two crawled from the hold.

———

"THAT'S RIGHT, Captain, six boxes of Sharps rifles marked Bibles and books. Each box holding about twenty rifles and several boxes of paper cartridges and that's enough to make quite a war," exclaimed Eli as he lifted his cup of steaming coffee for a sip. He looked over the rim at the captain, who sat shaking his head but did not slow his eating of the morning's breakfast.

The captain, his mouth full as he chewed on the last bite of breakfast biscuit, glanced up at Eli. With a shake of his head as he lifted his coffee, "We'll be comin' onto Fort Randall soon, the Woodhawks are usually upstream of the fort, since they cut every cottonwood within haulin' distance, and while we're loadin' firewood, perhaps you could take a ride back to Fort Randall and talk to the commandant and see if he wants to help with this problem."

"It's not just getting shut of the rifles that concerns me, Captain. I'd like to find out who's running the guns under the cover of a mission. If we just lose this shipment, there will be others, and a lot of soldiers and settlers will pay the price," explained Eli, frowning at the captain.

"I understand that, but as long as those rifles are aboard this boat, it endangers everyone!"

Eli chuckled, "If we unload 'em, what makes you think either the Sioux or the gunrunners will know they're no longer on board?"

"Well, for one thing, I believe those men at the table yonder," he glanced in the direction of the four men that were always together and seldom talked with anyone other than their group, "have somethin' to do with the shipment. And if we offload them, they'll know about it."

"And do what, Captain? Take the boxes from the military? There won't be any proof they're the ones that made the shipment, and no proof as to who they're going to or who's supposed to accept and deliver the rifles."

The captain continued with his breakfast, glancing to Eli as he ate and thought, "Well, we'll also stop near Fort Sully and Fort Rice, both within the boundaries of the Sioux territory. So, maybe we'll have some protection in case any renegades find out about the shipment and want to take it off our hands before..." he shrugged and reached for another biscuit.

———

IT WAS JUST after midday when the boat nosed into the sandy bank and dropped the gangplank. Eli and Twofer led the horses down the ramp and mounted up just as the wood hawks approached to make a deal with the captain. Putting the boat behind them, they rode into the fort which appeared more like a village than anything that resembled a fortification. Most of the structures were traditional stone or log construction, peaked roofs with split shingles, and were arranged around a central compound that held the traditional tall flagpole waving the red, white, and blue. Small carved signs directed visitors to the usual sutler, officer quarters, and commandant's office.

The two stepped down, slapped the reins around the hitchrail and stepped onto the covered boardwalk of the commandant's office and were promptly stopped by a burly sergeant who demanded, "What do you two want?!" as he scowled at the two men. He turned his attention to Eli and stood with hands on hips as he blocked the door to the office.

Eli chuckled, "At ease, Sergeant. Tell the commandant that Colonel Elijah McCain would like to see him."

The sergeant frowned, looking Eli up and down, and slowly relaxed, drawing himself to a more rigid stance but before he could salute, Eli stopped him, "Just let him know we're here."

"Yessir! Right away, sir!" replied the sergeant as he snapped a crisp salute and spun around to step through the door before Eli could return the salute.

Within a quick moment, the sergeant returned, saluted again, and said, "The major will see you, sir!" and stood with his salute held, awaiting the return salute from Eli.

Eli nodded, snapped a return salute, and stepped through the door, a confused Twofer following. Once inside, he stepped to the commandant's desk and noticing the nameplate on the desk, looked at the seated man, and said, "Major Mahana, thanks for taking time to see us."

"Certainly, is it Colonel McCain?"

"It is, or was, I've mustered out and am no longer on active duty. But there's something I need to talk to you about, it's a shipment of Beecher's Bibles."

The major frowned, "I haven't heard that expression for some time. Are we talking about the same kind of Bibles that earned that name?"

"We are," began Eli, as he began to explain about the shipment and the supposed destination of the boxes. He turned to Twofer and explained, "Twofer here wintered with Spotted Tail's Brulé, and they heard about the shipment bound for Red Cloud and his people. So, if the word has spread to the Brulé, I would suppose just about the whole Sioux nation and more might know about it."

"You say they're marked for Fort Benton?"

"They are, but like the captain said, anyone that meets them at any stop between here and there and have the proper papers, they'd be obligated to hand 'em over."

"So, you're thinking they'll try to take 'em off the boat before Benton?"

"If Red Cloud is expecting them, they'll need to be offloaded before we're out of Sioux territory."

"That's between here'n the Yellowstone, Fort Buford," mused the major.

Eli continued, "The captain would like to get rid of them sooner, but I'd like to find out who's doing the gunrunning and who's going to get them. But..." he paused, shaking his head, "I don't want to see them get into the hands of any of the Sioux."

"There's not a lot that we can do, our men are in the field, escorting some freighters and settlers west. They'll be back in a couple weeks, but we don't have any to spare, even if we were to follow the boat or board it." He dropped his chin onto his folded hands and looked at Eli, "The next post is Fort Sully, about two hundred miles north. Maybe they could spare some men to be on board or..." he shrugged as he looked at Eli.

"I understand, Major. It would be different if we knew what to expect and when, but..." Eli shrugged as he rose, prompting Twofer to stand as well. "We might stop at the sutler and get a few more rifles, ammunition, and such, just in case."

The commandant stood, extending his hand across the desk to shake, and said, "I wish we could do more, but bein' shorthanded as we are," he left the thought hang in the air between them, but shook hands and added, "Good luck to you!"

"Thanks, Major."

CHAPTER 22

LAKOTA

Heȟaka Sapa, Black Elk, sat across the small fire from *Matȟo Wanáȟtake*, Kicking Bear, glaring at him. "The white man said this land would be ours for 'as long as the river flows and the eagle flies,' but they lie and do not keep the treaty they forced upon our people. Now the white man comes with his many white-topped wagons and all their people. They kill our buffalo and destroy our land. Red Cloud is right, the white man does not want peace, they want our land and our lives. We must fight!"

"But Red Cloud and the other chiefs have gone to Fort Laramie to make another treaty! We should wait until they decide before we do anything that would break their words," declared Kicking Bear.

"If Red Cloud is waiting for the rifles, then he must be making words at the fort that are the same as the white man words and they mean nothing. He waits only for the time when he and his warriors have the white man's weapons. Why should we let the Oglala and Red Cloud get all the honors? If we take the rifles from the white man, we will be stronger than Red Cloud!"

"We do not know where the rifles are to be found," responded Bear.

"They are on one of the boats that come up the river!" explained Black Elk, shaking his head at the lack of understanding of Kicking Bear.

"There are many boats!" interjected *Sūŋkawakȟaŋ Sa*, Red Horse.

"I am told it is one with this," Elk picked up a stick and drew in the dirt the first letters of Louella.

"How do you know this?" asked Kicking Bear.

"*Ptehé Wóptuȟ'a*, the medicine man, Encouraging Bear."

The warriors looked at one another, and Bear said, "Then we must have more warriors."

"Yes," answered Black Elk, "We must get them now, and make ready to go to the river. We will make our plans when we return, then we will get the rifles and we will be the great warriors of the Brulé!"

Kicking Bear frowned at Black Elk, "The Minneconjou have warriors that would join us. When we went on the first hunt in the time of greening, Roman Nose, Frog, and Touch the Clouds, talked about the need for rifles, how they would make the hunt better and raids on the Pawnee or white men would bring greater honors and bounty."

"Then go to them, tell them to join us. We will meet here at the time of the new moon."

———

"RECKON YOU'NS'LL HAFTA MAKE it back to Benton on yore own this time!" declared Pug Witcher, cackling as he cracked the whip over the heads of the six-up of mules as they leaned into the harnesses, the heavy freight wagon creaking with the rough road.

"What'chu mean?" asked Jubal, sitting atop the cargo behind the driver's box.

"Ol' man Paquette axed fer volunteers to hang back an' wait fer a special cargo at the rapids. Said it was some boxes for the missionaries and needed to get to the fort right quick like, so, me'n Whittaker'll stay back till the *Louella* comes in and take them boxes on ahead, kinda special like." He poked Whittaker, his longtime partner, in the ribs as he chuckled. He leaned closer to Whittaker, supposing that Jubal could not hear as he added with a cackle, "An' we ain't gotta share that extry pay with 'em, neither!"

"That's alright by us," replied Jubal, looking back to his brother, "Ain't that right, Josh?" He leaned forward so he could be heard over the noise of the wagons, "We're headin' to the goldfields soon's we get back from this trip! Got a line on a good claim we can work on, mebbe buy it out, if'n it's any good."

"Gold! What'chu young'uns know 'bout diggin' gold?" growled Pug.

"Enough to know it pays better'n drivin' this thing!"

"How'd you hook up wit' gold diggers?"

"Talked to 'em at the poker table in the Last Chance. They was payin' with gold dust an' they had'm a big poke. Said they was needin' some help doin' the diggin' so they could get all the gold that they was. Said they'd pay us on shares!"

Pug and Whittaker sat silent, stewing and thinking, until Pug finally said, "Sounds like work to me. Ain't nuthin' like just sittin' up'chere and crackin' a whip an' lettin' the mules do all the work. Nosir, we'll just keep drivin' and makin' a little extry on the side. Ain't that right, Whit!?"

"Umm," grunted his partner, which was the usual response of the skinny helper.

———

"YOU LOOK LIKE YOU'RE GETTIN' ready to make war!" declared the captain as he watched Eli and Twofer lead the horses up the gangplank. The two men awkwardly carried an armload of rifles under one arm, had others tied on behind the saddles, several pistols in the saddlebags, and grinned at the captain as Eli responded, "You might say that."

The captain frowned and followed the men into the stall area and stood by as they stripped the gear from the horses, awaiting an explanation. "So, did you talk to the commandant of Fort Randall?"

"Did," answered Eli, reaching for a brush to give Rusty his usual rubdown.

"Well?" asked the slightly exasperated captain.

Eli chuckled, "He was no help. Suggested we try again at Fort Sully."

"And your armload of rifles?"

Eli paused, looked across the back of Rusty at the captain, "I got to thinkin' about what Twofer said and how the Brulé had heard about Red Cloud expecting to get some rifles, and if they know about it, then probably the entire Sioux nation knows about it. So, I thought if I was a young buck, lookin' for honors, thinkin' about impressing the girls, I'd be for makin' a try at getting the rifles. And if that's a possibility, I thought it might be in our best interest to have as many arms on board as we could, just to repel any possible attack."

"We have weapons for the crew, there are times we have to fight off Natives and outlaws, plus don't most folks have weapons of their own?" asked the captain, scowling at Eli.

"Many do, but just like the bunch I came on board with, there's a lot of these pilgrims only have old, musket loaders and sometimes useless rifles suitable only for taking a deer or such, not fighting off an attack. So, we brought a few of the newer repeaters, and we'll put 'em in the hands of those we think might be trustworthy and can hit what they aim at, you know, some of these fine ladies that learned how to shoot when their husbands were off to war, and a few farmers that never had a good rifle before. Folks that'll be happy to fight off any Native warriors that want to take their scalp and such."

"Well, for right now, how 'bout you keepin' 'em in your cabin and we'll decide together who should be trusted with those newfangled repeaters," declared the captain, turning on his heel and leaving, his frustration and anger showing.

Twofer looked at Eli, "Don't think he was too tickled 'bout you armin' the womenfolk. Hehehe," he cackled, rubbing down the grey as he looked over the back of the gelding to Eli.

"I'd rather have a mad captain than a dead one."

They felt the movement of the boat as the big paddle wheel churned the water and pulled the boat away from the shore. When the engine paused and the wheel stopped, the boat was moved by the current and the captain sounded the order with the bell and the boat began to move against the current, starting upstream. The nights had been clear, but the moon had waned into nothing more than a sliver of silver and offered little light for traveling on the uncertain and unpredictable Big Muddy. But Eli knew the captain would take advantage of every bit of light and would probably keep the boat on the move well into dusk before finally deciding to tie up and wait until morning. It was during those times that the boat would be most vulnerable, and Eli conferred with Twofer, "I know the captain is confident in his crew, but I've watched them. There was a fight 'fore you came aboard, and their best fighter...well, not the kind you'd want beside you in a real fight. I'm thinking we ought to recruit others for an additional watch, more than the usual crewmembers, as added precaution against the possible attack by the Natives."

Twofer nodded, "Ummhmm, an' we'll soon learn who's dependable an might know how to use them new rifles."

Eli grinned, nodding, "Exactly."

CHAPTER 23

WOODHAWKS

"So, how are you girls enjoying this grand adventure aboard a riverboat?" asked a smiling Eli, looking to the two Hamilton girls, Nora and Millie. The usual two families and more were seated at the table in the salon, taking the noon meal together.

Both girls smiled, the younger Millie giggling as Nora answered, "It has been quite an adventure, certainly!" She was doing her best to appear and sound more mature than her twelve years, glancing often to a neighboring table that had two boys of about her age seated with their parents.

Eli looked at Harriet, "And how's Mom doing?"

Harriet smiled, glanced to Constance Wellington who sat on the far side of Eli, "It has been a pleasant change from the miles on the wagon, that's for sure. But we're anxious for the miles to pass and we soon get to Fort Benton, and on to Helena." There was a touch of wistfulness in her voice and expression. Eli knew she was anxious to be reunited with her husband who was in the goldfields of Montana and the reason for their journey.

"So tell me, Harriet, in the many years on the farm, did you ever go hunting with your husband or have occasion to defend the home front?"

Harriet frowned, turned to look directly at Eli, "Yes, often, but why do you ask, Eli?"

Eli smiled, lifted his hand a little as if to stay her question as he turned to Constance, "And what about you, Constance, you don't impress me as a woman of the woods."

Constance dabbed at the corners of her mouth with her napkin, replaced it in her lap and with a slow smile, turned to Eli, "As if it were a matter of importance, I'll answer your question with a remark that no other man has heard, and that is yes, I am quite capable in the use of firearms. And as Harriet," nodding to the other woman, "asked, why the question?"

"First, let me ask the same question of Luther and Mildred, "So, Luther, are you well armed with a good rifle and, Mildred, have you ever used a rifle?"

Luther frowned and looked at Eli, "Yes, I am well armed. I have a Spencer rifle and a shotgun. As for Mildred, she has used the shotgun, but I did all the hunting."

"Well, Harriet, Constance, I don't believe you have rifles on board, but Ben," he looked to the oldest of Harriet's, "I know what you can do, and I have a rifle for you. But as to the reason," he lowered his voice and leaned forward, "we have reason to believe the boat might be attacked by a Sioux war party. There's cargo aboard that they want and might be willing to take the boat to get it.

"So we, Twofer and I, picked up some extra rifles, pistols, and ammunition when we were at Fort Randall, and we want everyone that can handle a rifle, to have one, on the off chance we may be right."

He looked around the table, "Now, don't go getting all alarmed, because we don't know for sure if, or when, or where, the Natives will attack. We might make it all the way to Fort Benton and never see a real live Indian. But, after we eat, I'll come to your," nodding to Harriet and Constance, "cabins with whatever you might need and will be comfortable with, and ammunition." He paused, looked from one to the other and continued, "I'll give each of you some guidance as what to do and when, so that if we are attacked, you'll know exactly what to do. You ladies will all remain in your cabins, and only come out through the door that opens into the salon. But if things turn bad, we might need your help. That's why I asked about your experience with rifles. Some just might need to reload for others," he paused, "like Maribel there. And if anyone is injured, you might be needed here in the salon to tend to the wounded."

He reached for his coffee cup, looked around at the others who seemed to be transfixed, and smiled as he added, "Now that I've scared the dickens out of all of you, just know, it might be nothing. So, in the meantime, let's enjoy the meal." He shrugged as he sat his coffee cup down and pulled his plate of food a little closer. His actions stirred the others, and they followed his example, but it was a few moments before conversation resumed.

Constance was the first to speak, "I guess that since the trip had been so comfortable and safe, we momentarily forgot that we are still in the Wild West. This is, after all, the land of the Natives and we should expect such things."

The others agreed and the conversation finally resumed some semblance of the normal discussions and remarks. Eli finished quickly, excused himself, and rose to leave. He looked at Constance and to Harriet, "I'll see you ladies shortly. First, there are some others I must talk with."

He went to the table where Chaplain Haney was dining with two other families. Eli wanted to visit with the group much like the conversation he just had with the Hamiltons and Williamses. When the chaplain saw him approach, he was waved over and introduced, "Folks, let me introduce an old acquaintance, Colonel Elijah McCain." He continued his introductions as he waved Eli to the nearby chair and explained their reunion. When Eli acknowledged each introduction, and the chaplain's tale, he grinned and began his query of the new families much like that with the others.

He talked with several others, not saying anything about the possibility of attack, but just getting to know them a little better. He had prided himself on being a good judge of character, after so many years in the military and needing to know those under his command, and his rounds of the tables and the promenade walkway, gave him a good idea of his fellow travelers. Although the four men that seemed to keep to themselves, managed to avoid any conversation with Eli and he chose not to force the issue. His suspicions of the four men had not tempered and he was determined to keep watch on their actions and acquaintances.

THE RIVER MADE a wide bend to the west and quickly bent back on itself as it rounded the point of a peninsula of land, just as they approached the mouth of the White River. The sun was kissing the western horizon as it foretold of the coming of dusk, just as the captain maneuvered the boat toward the sandy shore about a mile upstream of the confluence with the White. Eli was standing at the door of the pilothouse as the captain spun the big wheel and reached for the bell rope to signal the firemen below. He jerked the bell rope twice and the groan of the pitman shafts brought the paddle wheel to a halt as the boat nosed into the shore.

Above the low bank, a long stack of firewood beckoned, and several Woodhawks stood around, one at each end of the long stack, waving. Eli frowned as he looked at the waving men and looked closer at the few men below, "Wait, Captain, something's wrong."

The captain glanced to Eli, back to the woodyard, and said, "I don't see anything wrong."

"Look at those at the end of the stacks, they're only moving their arms and still waving. And those," pointing to those moving about closer to the shore, "they're all wearing moccasins! Those aren't white men, those are Indians!"

The captain grabbed the bell rope and jerked repeatedly to sound the alarm and get the fireman to engage the engines, but nothing happened. The boat coasted into the bank, nosing into the sloping sandy shore. The captain jerked on the rope again, heard the bells below, but still nothing happened.

Eli had carried his Winchester with him and lifted it to his shoulder, looking at the men on shore, but he heard a ruckus below and went to the edge to look over. He spotted two canoes tied off at the river side of the boat and knew instantly they had been boarded. He turned and hollered at the captain, "We've been boarded by Indians!" He ran to the port side and saw one of the men at the woodpile grab up a rifle and take aim at the boat, but Eli quickly lifted his rifle and took aim, squeezing off the first shot from the boat and dropping the man at the woodpile. That shot alarmed everyone else and everything busted loose.

Those on shore grabbed up their weapons and Eli started picking his targets, rifle fire from below told of a response on the lower decks, but he could not tell if it was from the passengers, crew, or boarders. The sounds of battle rattled through the boat and on the shore. Rifle fire, screams, whispers of arrows, shouts of alarm, shouted commands, and more gunfire. Eli picked each of his targets, knowing the necessity of not wasting the ammunition and making every shot count. He fired, jacked another round as he sought another target, fired again, moved to another position, continuing to fire as he moved.

He hollered at the captain, "Get us outta here!" and went to the stairs. A scream from below made him think of Constance and he took the steps two and three at a time. A painted warrior was coming up the lower stairs as he passed and Eli quickly snapped off a shot from his Winchester, taking the Indian in the chest and knocking him back down the steps, but Eli did not slow his step. He turned into the salon to see several warriors fighting with some of the men, but the sight of one dragging Constance from her cabin brought him around and he lunged at the man, bringing the butt of his rifle up to drive it into the face of the warrior, smashing his nose and jaw, knocking the man aside and loosing his grip on the woman.

Eli looked at Constance, who was struggling to her feet, and he lifted her up and looked at her, "Are you alright?"

She nodded, wide-eyed, and grabbed at the doorjamb

to steady herself. Eli quickly turned away and went to the aid of the fighters in the salon. He heard a gunshot behind him, turned to see Constance holding a smoking pistol, looking at the dead warrior at her feet. He brought the butt of the Winchester up in a tearing and ripping drive to split open the back of a warrior who screamed, arched his back and stumbled backward, as Eli jammed the barrel of the Winchester under the man's chin and pulled the trigger, blowing the top of the man's head off.

He turned, saw another warrior lifting his war axe to strike at the chaplain and quickly jacked another round into the chamber and fired from the hip, the bullet taking the warrior just below the armpit of his raised arm, and driving through the man's chest, to exit below his right clavicle, blowing a hole the size of a fist from his back. The war axe fell from his hand as his knees gave way and he crumpled to the floor. The chaplain nodded to Eli and turned to face another attacker.

Eli's attack and quick action turned the tide of the fight, and the men of the boat began to draw blood. Eli felt the boat begin to move, and with a glance to the door of Constance's cabin, saw it closed, he went to the promenade walk, saw a flood of warriors—mounted and afoot—charging down the slope toward the retreating boat. He looked around, took to the stairs to the lower main deck and saw Twofer fighting with a warrior, but before he could get to him, the old mountain man drove his big knife into the warrior's gut, twisted it side to side, and watched as the man's eyes flared, blood came from his mouth, and he fell to the deck. Twofer stepped back, wiped his knife on the warrior's buckskins, and looked for another target. He saw Eli, looked about, and seeing no one close, started toward his friend, but Eli stepped to the rail and began firing at those on shore that were trying to get to the boat before it moved into deep water. Two men were swimming, but the bullets from Eli and Twofer sunk their carcasses below the waves.

The two men looked at one another, then to the retreating shore and shook heads and without a word, went separate ways around the main deck, looking for boarders.

CHAPTER 24

PURSUIT

The chug of the engines and the creak of the big pitman shafts began turning the paddle wheel and the boat slowly turned into the current. Sporadic rifle fire and random arrows rattled the rails and siding of the boat; most of the passengers and crew had taken cover with an occasional shot coming from on board toward the scattered attackers on shore. The sun had tucked itself behind the western horizon and the dim light of dusk was rapidly fading, but the captain's familiarity with the river's course showed its worth as the boat moved away from the attack site.

Eli returned to the pilothouse, the captain busy at the wheel, but Eli gave an update. "We had two passengers killed, both single men on the main deck, killed when the Sioux boarded on the starboard side. Three others were wounded, one by an arrow, two in the fight in the salon, one took a bad stab from a knife, might not make it. The other had his ear sliced off with a tomahawk, but that Indian won't do that again. The wounded are in the salon, women tending to 'em." He paused, looking at the river with starlight dancing off the ripples, and added, "Your Mate had the crew moppin' up and throwing the bodies of the Sioux overboard." He looked at the stoic captain, "Are you gonna make it very far in this light?"

The captain chuckled, "I know this stretch, good channel, shouldn't have any trouble. But..." he looked at Eli, "if those Sioux decide to follow and hit us again, it'll probably be about twenty miles north. The river cuts back on itself and we'll have to make over twenty miles around the bend, but across land, it's only 'bout twenty miles to that point and only a couple miles between the crooks of the bend. If *I* was plannin' an attack, that'd be where *I'd* hit."

"How far is it to that cutback?" asked Eli.

"'Bout twenty miles."

"And that'd take us about three, four hours?"

"About that, yeah."

"And on land, they could do that in less than three, if they tried hard," mused Eli. He looked at the captain, "That's why I preferred the cavalry, easy to move about and hard to corner."

The captain nodded, "We do pass Fort Thompson 'tween here and there, at the mouth of Soldier Creek, but it's on the east side and they've been building and such. Reckon the commandant is one of those desk soldiers and is more intent on building really big stockade walls to hide behind. Seldom see any of 'em leave the fort, and from what I hear, the major in charge sees his duty is to the settlers and on that side of the river only, so, I don't think they would be much help."

Eli pondered the information for a moment, "Then I reckon I might see what I can do to get folks prepared. It'll still be dark when we get to that cutback, but..." he paused a moment, looked up at the captain, "and those four men that we thought might be the runners? I didn't see them doin' much during the attack. If the Indians hadn't gotten into the salon, I don't think they would have ever left, but they ganged up on one of 'em, did him in and threw him overboard."

"Then they weren't entirely useless?"

"Not entirely, but I'm still skeptical and suspicious," responded Eli, turning away and starting for the lower decks. He looked for Twofer, finding him stretched out on a cargo box covered with a buffalo robe and snoring like a warped two-man saw. Eli chuckled as he grabbed the man's foot and shook him awake.

"Wha..wha...Oh, it's you. Now what?" he grumbled, sitting up and rubbing the sleep from his eyes. He snarled as he looked at Eli, his vague figure visible in the darkness.

"We need to talk."

"So, talk. I ain't got no secrets."

With a nod of his head, Eli left the makeshift bed and walked to the rail at the side of the boat and waited for his friend. When the grumbling mountain man sided him, Eli relayed the information from the captain about his suspected location for another attack.

"Sounds likely. It'll still be dark but with dawn comin' they'd pr'oly give it a try at a place like that. If that cutback is like I'm thinkin' they'd hit first at the beginnin' of the bend, hurry round to the other point an' hit again, prob'ly try boardin' then, or maybe from canoes." He frowned, thinking, and looked at Eli, "Oh, an' I was gonna tell ya', I recognized a couple them fellas, one of 'em was a Brulé name o' Kickin' Bear. He was allus wantin' to be a war leader and was allus makin' trouble an' big talk. I also recognized one fella name o' Touch the Clouds. Onliest thing is, he's a Minneconjou, an' that means all them Teton Sioux is gettin' together and that means an almighty big war."

"I thought that was too big a bunch to just be a war party of young bucks an' renegades," responded Eli, shaking his head as he looked at the shadowy riverbank that slowly passed. "And unless they're attackin' any and all riverboats, they must know the cargo we're carryin'."

"Ummhmmm. An' that means the onliest way o' gettin' word ahead of us that fast, is some white man used the tellygraph, told his cohorts, and they passed word to Red Cloud an' his boys, an' on an' on' it goes."

"Worse'n two ol' women gossipin' o'er the back fence," grumbled Eli, shaking his head and kicking at the bottom rail.

He continued, "You keep a guard or two out all night, let folks get some rest but if they stir an' such, let 'em know what might be comin'. The women are tendin' the wounded in the salon, but the captain'll have a guard or two up top and I'll prob'ly be rovin' around too." He paused, looked from the water and back at Twofer, frowned and added, "Might wanna keep a check on the access to the hold, I got a suspicion 'bout that."

"Will do, Colonel sir!" declared Twofer, snapping a mock salute and a sneaky grin as he finished with his usual, "Hehehehe."

———

ELI WAS NOT surprised to see Constance and Harriet seated together at a small table, each one nursing a steaming cup of coffee. They looked up as he entered and both smiled as he stepped to the table, "May I join you, ladies?" he asked, his hand resting on the back of the single unoccupied chair.

Constance nodded, "Certainly, sir."

Eli had looked around the salon and saw no wounded on the tables and asked, "The wounded?"

"We had them double up in a cabin, there," answered Constance, nodding to one of the cabins on the starboard side. "the one with the arrow wound is doing well, the one that lost his ear is struggling, lots of pain, but they both should be fine. The one with the knife wound didn't make it. We had the crew remove his body."

"Friends, family?" asked Eli.

"The one with the arrow wound, Mr. Proctor, had a brother, the man with the knife wound. But the man with the head wound, well, he hasn't made much sense, and no one has asked about him. The man that died was going to the goldfields to make his fortune and then he was going to find himself a wife." Constance looked at Harriet and both women frowned and dropped their eyes to the coffee.

"Well, I was talking with the captain, and he explained about a point in the river upstream that might be the site of another attack. It's about three to four hours away, so, I think it would be good for you ladies to get some rest. You might be needed again."

"Is it always going to be like this, Eli? I mean, the constant attacks from the Indians and such?" pleaded Harriet, fear showing in her eyes.

"Not always, Harriet. Right now, the Natives are angry because the treaty made by the government has not been kept. They were promised their land 'as long as the river flows and the eagle flies' and the army was to keep the white men from taking their land. The tribes agreed to let the settlers pass, but not to settle and kill off the buffalo. And the government promised to pay an annuity and give supplies so the Natives would not have to raid and steal, but the politicians have again failed to honor their promises. Now, I know that shouldn't be a surprise, but the Indians put great value in keeping your word, and even though the treaty was signed and agreed to, it did not last. Now," he paused, took a drink of coffee, "the leaders of several nations, the Sioux, Crow, Arikara, Blackfeet, and more, are meeting at Fort Laramie to make another treaty, but obviously the Natives are skeptical. While the chiefs are at Fort Laramie, their warriors are making attacks and raids to get honors, scalps, booty, and more. Mainly, they want to get the guns of the white men that will make the balance of war tip in their favor."

"But, that's terrible. The ones that pay with their lives are the settlers and soldiers," pleaded Harriet.

"And there are many women in their hide lodges that are grieving because they believe that the ones that pay with their lives are their sons."

"Oh," muttered Harriet, putting her hand to her mouth as her eyes filled with sadness, pouring out in tears.

"And just like among the whites, there are those Native leaders that don't want war but are trying for peace. Twofer wintered with a band of the Brulé, led by the chief named Spotted Tail, who does not want war of any kind and refuses to join the leader of the Oglala, Chief Red Cloud, as he calls for war. You see, the Sioux have what they call the Seven Council Fires that oversees the nation of Sioux. But they split into the Lakota and the Dakota, each having several different bands among them. We are in Lakota territory, the land of the Brulé, Oglala, Minneconjou, and others. The Sioux fight the Pawnee, who live back in the Nebraska Territory, and the Crow, whose land lies between us and Fort Benton. But, they have also allied with the Cheyenne and the Arapaho, both tribes that fought the white man's incursion into their treaty lands in Colorado Territory. So, you see, it can get confusing, for just like white men have people from the north and south that fought each other, even among those are smaller groups that fight, like the Bushwhackers, guerrillas, Red Legs, and more." He grinned as he looked to the two women, "Confusing, isn't it?"

Harriet took a deep breath that lifted her shoulders and shook her head, "It's true then, that the only real peace is the peace that comes from God."

CHAPTER 25

CUTBACK

"That's Fort Thompson," stated the captain, nodding to the right on the northeast bank of the river. "It's at the mouth of Soldier Creek, only been there a couple years, but looks to be like they're gonna be makin' the stockade bigger."

"I know it's dark and all, but it doesn't have any sign of life. Don't they post guards?" asked Eli, frowning as he looked at the big dark shadow.

"I wouldn't know. I'm not, nor ever have been, a soldier. So, I dunno just what they should be doin'." He nodded forward, "Now, it's only 'bout four miles to the beginning of the big bend. The channel hugs the north or east bank and that'll probably put us outta bowshot for the Sioux, but they got a few rifles and might take a potshot or two. But," he took a deep breath and cocked his head to the side a mite, "on the far side of those hills is the cutback, and the channel there hugs the south bank as it comes around, and that will be within range of their bows and anything else they got!"

"Is the water such that they could come at us from the far side with canoes?" asked Eli.

"Yup."

"Trees for cover for 'em?"

"Yup."

"How wide's the river there?"

"Half mile, 'bout like this," nodding to the river before them, explained the captain.

"And it'll take about a couple hours or so to get around the bend?"

"That's right. You could prob'ly get out and hoof it o'er those hills yonder and be waiting on the bank for us by the time we'd get there."

"But that's where you think the Indians'll be waitin'."

"If they're anywhere, that's where I'd expect 'em," answered the captain.

Eli looked about, seeing the river, the movement of the boat, the dark shadows on the shore and pondered. He stepped out of the pilothouse, looked at the starlit sky, the Milky Way, and the moon that was waxing to first quarter. He looked at the rolling hills that fled from the river, stretching out into the flats. He guessed the hills to the east rose about two to three hundred feet above water level, and the plains stretched away, catching the light of the moon and holding it as it lay on the grassy flats. He looked up again, the moon almost straight overhead and the dim shadows from its muted light beginning to stretch to the east. *When we make it around the bend, that light will be on the west-facing bank and the south bank, and what light there is will be to our backs. That'll be to our advantage.*

"Captain, did I see the prow of a canoe back of the crew's quarters?"

"You did. That is my birchbark canoe, traded from the

Mohawk on the upper Mississippi."

"Here's what I'm thinkin', Captain..." began Eli, detailing his freshly conjured plan for the possible attack. He detailed the work aboard and the placement of shooters as well as the preparation of the women to tend to any wounded. When he finished, the captain nodded, "Sounds good, but I hope you know, not everything goes according to plan."

"But the better the plan, and simpler, the more likely we'll have success. And after what Twofer said about there being more than one band of the Sioux involved, there's no telling how many will be waiting for us."

Eli left the Texas deck and returned to the main deck, looking for Twofer. When he spotted the whiskery faced old-timer, he waved him over and began detailing his plan. "Now, we'll need to pick our shooters, and even 'em out on both sides, because I'm certain they'll try coming from the river side as well as the shore side."

Twofer grinned, remembering, "Like they did last time. Get us busy on the shore side, an' sneak aboard from the river?"

"Right. You take care of the main deck, space out your shooters, and I'll do the same for the Hurricane deck. The captain will get the mate to do the same on the Texas deck. Then I'll meet you on the starboard side after we round the point of the bend. The boat will be coming closer to the south side with the hills, captain says that's where the main channel is, and we'll be on the far side."

"Ya' say we got 'bout a couple hours?"

"Little less."

"See ya' then," drawled Twofer and with a nod, started to move among the many passengers on the main deck.

Eli climbed the stairs to the cabin, or Hurricane deck,

and went first into the salon. Even the card players and gamblers had turned in and the salon was empty. He went to the lantern sconces, lit several, and then started door to door to roust everyone out. As the sleepy-eyed passengers dragged themselves into the salon, most griping and complaining, they found chairs or sat on the tables or leaned against the walls. Eli began, "Folks, the captain thinks we might be attacked again by the Natives. If so, it'll probably be in a little more than an hour. We'll be coming around a sharp bend and will be close to the shore, close enough they can easily fire into the boat, and even make it on board. But, here's what we need to do..."

"But I thought that was the crew's job, to protect us!" whined a skinny older man standing in his pajamas, his robe hanging loosely around his shoulders and his thinning hair almost standing on end.

"They'll do their job. But we have reason to believe there are several bands of the Sioux that want to take this boat, take supplies and cargo, as well as kill their share of white men."

"Boss, do that mean they won't kill us'ns?" drawled a mischievous colored man that was the steward of the coloreds that worked in the galley and other places.

Eli chuckled, "I wish it were that easy, Shamus." He continued with his plan, detailing the placement of the shooters and the plan to tend to the wounded and more.

"And what about you? Where you gonna be?" asked one of the men that Eli recognized as one of the four men that always kept to themselves and that he suspicioned as part of the gunrunners.

"I'll be about. And I'll be doing my part, and more, don't you worry," explained Eli. With more mumbles and grumbles, the crowd broke up and went to their cabins to get dressed and ready for the coming battle. Eli shook his head as he watched them disperse and motioned for Benjamin to join him. He looked at the young man, "I'm going to need you with me. We'll be coming at things from a different direction. Get your Spencer and ammunition and meet me up on the Texas deck by the pilothouse."

Benjamin broke into a broad grin and said, "Yessir! Right away, sir!"

ELI AND BENJAMIN silently dropped the birchbark canoe down to the next deck, and finally into the water beside the boat. Twofer leaned over to hold it in place as first Benjamin and then Eli stepped in and seated themselves. Twofer made a long stretch and dropped into the canoe, picking up the paddle as he was seated. Eli spoke as softly as possible, "Let's stay near the far shore, in the shadow of the trees, but keep up with the boat." Only Eli and Twofer paddled, and Eli told Benjamin, "Make yourself as comfortable and as low as possible and check your rifle. Make sure you're loaded up and ready. When we open fire, we'll all be shooting and doing it as fast and as accurate as we can. But you just take your time and pick your shots. Better to hit 'em than try to scare 'em."

"Will there be very many?" asked the curious lad.

"Enough. But don't shoot until we do, got that?"

"Yessir."

They dipped the paddles deep and moved as silently as possible, knowing there would probably be some Sioux waiting in the shadows for the riverboat, and their attention would be focused on the big boat. Twofer lifted his paddle high to signal Eli to stop paddling. Both men froze in place, listening and trying to penetrate the darkness as they watched and listened. The big boat chugged along, dark smoke spewing with a few glowing embers from the tall smokestacks. Pale blue moonlight was bouncing off the waves and making the monster boat glow in the night.

Three canoes slipped silently from the shadows before them, oars dipping into the ripples and pulling the canoes across the water. Eli counted five or six in each canoe, and Twofer slowly dipped his paddle and started pulling against the current. They counted on the warriors keeping their attention on the big boat, never thinking about what might come from behind, and all the canoes slipped across the waves, drawing closer to the big paddle-wheeler.

As it started its turn to the north around the last crook of the cutback bend, the big boat was broadside to the canoes and someone on board shouted, "Here they come!" and fired the first shot. Twofer had warned everyone that they would also be in a canoe, and to be careful where they shot, but he was not counting on their discretion for a man's judgment in the midst of an Indian attack can be distorted, at best, and missing entirely, at worst.

The Indians screamed their war cries and opened fire. Those with rifles had been placed in the middle of the canoes while the paddlers could control the craft before taking up their bows. As they fired their first volley, the shooters in the canoes struggled to reload their musket rifles and Eli spoke to Twofer, "Whenever you're ready!" Twofer lay the paddle alongside his leg and lifted his Spencer. He eared back the hammer and said, "Now!" as he pulled the trigger. The hammer dropped and the rifle bucked, as it spat lead, but Ben and Eli fired their rifles at about the same time and the resulting roar startled the Sioux.

The warriors in the canoes screamed the alarm and Eli saw them scrambling in the small space but showed no mercy and jacked round after round through his Winchester and dealt death with every bullet. Twofer lay down a steady volley and Benjamin, lying low in the canoe and using the gunwale to steady his aim, fired repeatedly and soon realized he could do better without using the gunwale. He was one of the few that had a natural aim and good eye for shooting and he sat up, lifted a knee, and used it to steady himself, then fired and fired again, continuing as the two others kept up their barrage.

Twofer lowered his empty rifle and quickly grabbed another cylinder with seven more cartridges and emptied it into the magazine. He soon lifted his rifle to continue the barrage. All the while, the Winchester in Eli's hands blasted away with its .44 Henry cartridges, all fourteen of them. When he lowered his rifle to reload, both Benjamin and Twofer were blasting away. He looked at the canoes alongside the big boat and nothing moved. Every warrior had been shot down or had taken to the water to escape.

Eli said, "We're done here. But it sounds like they're still shootin' on the far side. Let's come alongside and get back aboard!"

"Gotcha!" answered Twofer, laying his rifle on the seat beside him and picking up the paddle to maneuver alongside the boat. He hollered up, "Hey! It's me, Twofer, and we're comin' back aboard! Don't go shootin'!" They quickly slipped alongside, climbed aboard, and grabbed the birchbark from the water and lay it on deck before going to the port side to help finish the fight.

With a nod to one another, Twofer and Eli went in separate directions and Eli sent Ben up the stairs to the cabin deck, "Go into the salon, your ma and Constance might need some protection if they're helping the wounded."

As Eli started around the bow, he stopped dead in his tracks when he saw the hatch cover to the hold was pushed aside. Standing beside the skewed cover was one of the four men, a Sioux warrior beside him. As Eli watched, an armload of Sharps rifles lifted up from the opening and the Sioux reached down to accept the rifles. Eli looked to see other warriors watching and waiting as the first bunch of rifles appeared, their excitement and anticipation growing. Eli eared back the hammer on his Winchester, aimed for the man in the hold reaching up with the armload of rifles and fired. The blast of the rifle startled the others as each of the warriors dropped into a crouch, searching for the source of the shot, but Eli's next bullet took the white man in the chest, and he fell into the opened hold.

The Indians screamed and charged toward the shooter, but Eli jacked another round and fired again and again, dropping two more warriors, but two others charged, the first with a raised tomahawk. Eli's rifle was knocked aside as the big warrior screamed and lifted his hawk to strike again, but Eli snatched his pistol from the holster, cocking it as he brought it up jamming it into the man's gut and pulled the trigger. The pistol roared and spat flame and lead, the bullet burrowing its way through the man's gut and shattering his backbone, making the warrior fall at Eli's feet. But the second warrior lifted his musket and dropped the hammer. The big rifle exploded with a cloud of grey smoke and a piercing tongue of fire as it launched its lead ball toward

Eli. The bullet took him in the side, just below his heart and Eli staggered back, his legs losing their strength and he dropped to his knees to see the warrior raise his long rifle like a club, but a gun from the promenade on the second deck roared and the bullet exploded the face of the warrior, driving him to his back where he kicked once and lay still.

Eli snatched up his Winchester, and rose to his feet, leaning against the rail. He looked up at the second deck to see Benjamin, leaning over the rail, grinning as he held the Spencer carbine with a tendril of smoke coming from the muzzle. "You alright?" shouted the young man.

"Yeah! Thanks to you!" Eli looked around, moved to the hatch cover, and kicked it back in place and started around the edge of the stacked cargo. Sporadic gunfire still racketed, the sounds echoing back from the jagged bluffs at river's edge. He spotted a warrior pulling himself up from the water, and Eli shot him in the face, bloodying the water as he fell back into the river. He searched for another target, saw others climbing from the water onto the shore and making their escape among the rocky bluffs. Some of the shooters aboard the boat still took potshots at the escapees, but few found their mark.

Twofer saw Eli stumble and lean against a pillar of the railing, and stepped beside his friend, saw the blood at his side, "We better git you to the womenfolk, let 'em patch that up."

"Then give me a hand, or at least carry my rifle."

"Gimme that thar rifle 'fore you try usin' it as a crutch! Won't do you no good to get the muzzle plugged and have it blow up on ya'!" chuckled Twofer and he reached for the rifle to let Eli have both hands free to hold the rail and make it up the stairs.

CHAPTER 26

RESOLUTION

"You think they'll hit us?" asked Ramon Valdez, as he looked at the leader of the crew, Skip Martin.

"Wouldn't you if you wanted to get the rifles in those cargo boxes? They see the rifles as their only way to win against the soldier boys." He chuckled as he grinned at the others, "But if they take 'em without us gettin' paid, well, we can't be havin' that."

"What if we could make a deal with 'em?" asked Bert Wolff, who considered himself the number two of their group.

"Oh, so you expect 'em to just stop in the middle of an attack and sit down and talk trade?" he forced a laugh, shaking his head at the stupidity of the men. He looked at the three that sat at the table with him and knew between the three they might have one brain, but it wasn't their brain he was concerned about, he would do the thinking. But he needed them for their brawn and their guns. He knew that anytime you have to deal with the Sioux or any other tribe, it would be dangerous, but could also be very rewarding. His deal with Red Cloud was for him to deliver six boxes of rifles in exchange for the location of gold. He knew there were places in the territory of the Natives that were untouched and likely held rich pockets of gold, and he also knew the Natives, although they never mined the gold, when it was available, they would use the nuggets to make jewelry like armbands, wristlets, necklaces and more for themselves and their women. His plan was to high-grade those pockets and hightail it with their packs full of gold before any of the troops would find out they were in Indian Territory.

Skip Martin frowned, looked at his second in command, and said, "You know, that might not be a bad idea. Look..." he leaned forward, his shoulders hunched over the table and dipped his finger in the mug of beer and began to draw on the tabletop, "this is where the captain thinks the attack will come, but the river makes a wide bend like this..." and he continued to lay out his plan for Ramon to meet with the Sioux and explain about the rifles and how they could get them.

"So, how do I get ashore?" asked Ramon.

"You can swim, can'tchu?" suggested Skip, chuckling. "And you can come back onboard with the Sioux, and we'll have a man in the hold getting the rifles and ready to hand 'em off. That way, we can make a deal with this bunch, and still have rifles left for Red Cloud."

CONSTANCE, Harriet, and Mildred had recruited another woman to help with the wounded. There were five tables and six wounded and Constance seemed to be the woman in charge, giving directions and help to the others. When she looked up and saw Eli holding a bloody hand to his side, her eyes flared and she hollered at two men standing by, "Get that table over here!"

The men quickly responded to the order and pulled the table near the others for Constance to spread a blanket over the top. She looked from Eli to Twofer and ordered, "You, whisker face, help him up on this table!"

Eli and Twofer both chuckled and the mountain man leaned their rifles against the end of the table and gave Eli a hand getting atop the table and held tight to his arm as he lay back. Constance came near and began grabbing at his shirttail and pulled it from his britches, unbuttoning it and opening the shirt wide to expose the wound. She grabbed some bits of cloth that had been lain aside for bandages and wiped the wound clean. She motioned to Twofer to help her roll him to his side so she could look at the back and satisfied it was a through and through, she began cleaning and tending to the wound.

When she finished, she gave Eli a stern look, "Now, you'll have to mind me and let me take care of that, so it'll heal proper. If you don't, it'll get infected, and you'll play hob getting better!"

Eli chuckled, winced at the pain, and answered, "Yes, ma'am. Now help me up so you can tend to the others."

Constance smiled, gave him her hand, and helped him sit up and drop his legs over the edge of the table. As he buttoned his shirt, he looked around the salon, seeing who was wounded and who might be missing. He frowned when he recognized Luther Williams on one of the tables, with Mildred at his side. He apparently had more than one wound and Eli looked at Constance, "Is Luther alright?"

Constance dropped her eyes to some bandages on the

table, "He took a bullet to his head and an arrow to his middle. I don't think he'll make it."

Eli frowned, looked from Constance to Mildred and walked to the table where Luther lay. Luther looked at Eli, "I done my part with muh Spencer!" and tried to force a smile but winced at the pain, "I reckon it's good I have such a hard head," and lifted his hand to the bandage.

"You did indeed do your part and more. I s'pect you showed those Sioux what a midwestern farmer can do with a Spencer," answered Eli, taking Luther's hand.

Luther looked at his friend, motioned him closer and spoke softly, "If'n I don't make it, will you see to muh family?"

"I will. But it'd be better if you quit jawin' and put all that effort into getting better. Now you need to show these nursemaids what a midwestern farmer is made of and get better right quick!" explained Eli, grinning at his friend as he clasped his hand tighter.

Luther nodded, closed his eyes, and relaxed. Eli released his hand and stepped away, allowing Mildred to take his place at Luther's side. Maribel, Mildred's daughter and Benjamin's sweetheart, had joined in the work of nursing the wounded and willingly took Mildred's place. Eli went to Constance, "Don't you think they'd be more comfortable in their cabins?"

"Yes, and we can move them, but some don't have cabins, they're from the main deck."

Eli motioned to a couple men that were standing along the wall, sipping on a much-needed cup of coffee and as they came near, "How 'bout you fellas help the ladies get these wounded back into their cabins. There are a couple of 'em from down below and I'll see if I can get the captain to give 'em a cabin or someplace so they'll be a little more comfortable. You fellas can start, I'll be right back."

When Eli stepped into the pilothouse, the captain was standing at the forward window while the pilot manned the wheel. "Captain, we've got some wounded that could use a better bunk, maybe in a cabin. You have any empties?"

Captain Marsh looked at the pilot, "You know of any empties?"

"Nope, but your Mate, Fleming, might."

Eli had a thought, "You know those four men we suspected?"

"Yeah, what about 'em?"

"There's only two of 'em now, I caught the other two passing rifles to the Sioux and had to put a stop to it. So, did they have a cabin?"

The captain frowned, slowly shook his head as he grabbed the ledgers and scanned the pages, "Ummhmm, they had two cabins – eighteen and nineteen. Don't know who was in which one, but..." he shrugged, looking up at Eli. "Do the others know what happened?"

"If not, they soon will," replied Eli, turning away, and taking to the stairs to return to the salon.

Cabins eighteen and nineteen were the last cabins on the starboard side and butted up to the galley. As Eli came down the stairs, he noticed two of the men standing at the rail outside cabin nineteen and naturally assumed cabin eighteen had been occupied by the two men he caught passing rifles to the Sioux and whose bodies still lay in the hold. He went into the salon, saw Constance and Harriet already had the men move four of the six into their cabins, and stood beside the last two. "Bring those two this way," motioning toward the now empty cabin. He opened the door to cabin eighteen, stepped inside and gathered up an armload of things—clothing and such, left behind, to make way for the two wounded men to take the empty bunks.

The outside door of the cabin opened and the leader of the four men stood wide-eyed, "Hey! What do you think you're doin'? This cabin is taken. My friends are in this cabin. Get outta here 'fore I hafta throw you out!" demanded Skip Martin, scowling at the men handling the makeshift stretchers and the two women.

Eli spoke up from behind them, "This cabin is empty! The captain said to put these wounded in here since the two men that were in here are dead!"

"What do you mean, dead?! They ain't dead! They were here just a little bit ago!" protested Martin, looking from Eli to the last of his men, Bert Wolff, who shrugged his shoulders and held out empty hands to show he knew nothing.

"Dead, you know, like they were shot and were killed. You know, it happens quite often when a war party of Natives attack folks."

Martin scowled and growled, "Don't get smart with me or you might end up dead! Now, where are they and what happened?" The leader of the gunrunners stood in the doorway, his hand resting on the butt of his holstered pistol on his hip as he stared at Eli.

"They were caught passing rifles to the Sioux and I shot 'em, and had to discourage the Sioux also. You know, by killing several of their warriors so they couldn't get any of those rifles. You know, the ones in the cargo boxes marked Bibles!?"

"I don't know anything about that, but those were friends of mine, and I don't think they were doin' what you said. You've been all high and mighty prancin' around here, barkin' your orders like you were somebody special and you ain't nuthin' to me!"

As the intruder growled his challenge, the women and stretcher bearers backed out of the room as Eli motioned for them to leave. When the room emptied, Eli said, "I don't have to explain myself to the likes of you and when you start talkin' like that, it's the same as calling me a liar, and that just kinda sticks in my craw. So..." Eli had crossed his arms which placed his right hand just above the butt of his Colt Army .44. He also had his Bowie knife in the scabbard at his back and the LeMat pistol tucked into his belt at the small of his back. He had armed himself well when he and Twofer had taken to the canoe. "Now, you can back out of that door, close it behind you, and go about your business, or..." he shrugged.

Skip Martin had been in enough scrapes to recognize this man had no backup in him and with that expression, he looked like he was anxious for a fight. He also knew the odds were not in his favor, it had been his way to make sure the odds tipped his way, usually made so by having others in the fight to cover him and eliminate any possibility of failure. But if the other two were dead, that left just Bert to back him, and he was not in any position to do that. Skip's nostrils flared as he lowered his hand away from his pistol and slowly backed out, closing the door between them.

Eli turned back, exited the cabin, and closed the door. With a nod to the women who were partaking of a much-needed cup of coffee, he decided to join them. As he neared, "You ladies have done so much, thank you." He sat down and poured himself a cup and leaned back in the chair.

Constance looked at him, "So, what was that all

about?" nodding toward the cabin where the confrontation took place.

Eli chuckled and began to explain about the rifles and the reason the Sioux had attacked the boat and his suspicions of the four men being the gunrunners. "And when I found the two of them trying to pass the rifles to the Indians, my suspicions were confirmed. When they were about to hand off the rifles, I put a stop to it and the Natives did not like that, so they tried to kill me. That's when I took a bullet."

"But what about them?" asked Harriet, nodding in the direction of the cabin.

"Dunno. We have no proof that all of them were involved, but I'm sure they were. I think the captain is planning on stopping at Fort Sully and maybe turn them over to the military."

"But if the Indians think we still have the rifles, won't they attack again?" asked Constance.

"Dunno, maybe. But they've taken considerable losses and they're smart enough to know that rifles won't be any good if you don't have the warriors to use them." Eli took a sip of his coffee and saw Benjamin coming into the salon, frowning, and looking around.

"What's the matter, Ben? You look like you lost something," asked Eli.

"Have you seen Maribel?" asked the young man, looking at the women.

"She was here just a little bit ago, but we haven't seen her in the last few minutes. She probably went to her cabin, her dad was wounded and she's probably with him," offered Constance.

"No, she's not there. They haven't seen her, and she was supposed to meet me on the promenade walk back by the paddle wheel, but she's not there." He looked around as he spoke, obviously concerned.

Eli stood, "I'll go with you, and we'll find her." He looked at the ladies, tipped his hat, "Ladies—thanks again!"

CHAPTER 27

HOSTAGE

"So, what're we gonna do now?" grumbled Bert Wolff as he stared at Skip Martin.

"We can't be stayin' here, they'll try to turn us over to the army when we get to Fort Sully," growled Skip, leaning on the rail of the promenade outside their cabin. They were at the stern of the boat, the end of the promenade walkway. Skip leaned over to look below, saw the prow of the birchbark canoe that had been hastily stashed by Eli and Twofer. He looked down the promenade walk and saw a young woman, girl really, standing alone. As he looked, Eli and Benjamin came from the salon, onto the promenade and the young man called out to the girl.

Neither Ben nor Eli had noticed the two men standing behind them on the promenade as Ben rushed to Maribel's side. "Where you been? I've been lookin' ever'where for you!" Before she could answer, he turned back to Eli, "Thanks, Eli, you can tell her ma we found her."

Eli chuckled, nodded, and turned back to the door

into the salon. He noticed the two men standing together and recognized them as the two remaining gunrunners, but he did not want to have another confrontation until he talked with the captain. He went through the door, pulling it closed behind him.

Skip turned back to Bert, grinning, "I know what we'll do. Let's go into the cabin and get our gear, and I'll explain."

———

"DID YOU FIND HER?" asked Constance when Eli returned to the table to have some more coffee.

He chuckled and smiled, "She was just outside on the promenade. They're together now and they're both a bit happier."

"They're a nice couple," said Constance as she turned to Harriet, "And that boy of yours is sure turning into a fine young man!"

Harriet laughed and smiled proudly, "He's so much like his dad, and he's done so much since Cyrus left for the goldfields. He stepped up to be the man of the home and I'm very proud of him."

"Well, he was a help during the fight with the Sioux," declared Eli. "He did as much as any man on board and more than most. If it hadn't been for him, I might not have made it. When those warriors attacked after we came back aboard and I took a bullet, that warrior was about to split my skull and Ben shot him from the deck above us. He saved my life."

"Oh my!" declared Harriet, "I didn't know. He shot a man?"

"No, he didn't just shoot a man, he shot the warrior

that was trying to kill me. And before that he helped as we stopped the attack from the far side, and he did his share of shooting too. He did what any good man would do, and more than most. He's not a boy any longer, he's a man."

They were interrupted when the door slammed open and Twofer stormed in shoutin', "They took 'em! They took 'em!"

Eli stood and looked at the whiskery old man, "Whoa up there, Twofer. Who took what?"

"Them two no-good, lying, stealin', gun-runnin' outlaws! That's who! An' they done took Ben and his girlfriend!"

Eli frowned, "What? No, they were just outside!"

"Yeah, they're outside alright. They took the captain's birchbark and put them two in the middle, held a gun to her head so I couldn't shoot 'em, an' said we'd get 'em back when we turned over them 'Bibles'!"

Harriet stood beside Eli, her hand at her mouth, eyes wide and fear dancing in her eyes as she stammered, "Oh my God, no! Eli, you've got to get my boy back, please!" she pleaded, grabbing at Eli's sleeve as she grew faint and began to crumple. Constance was beside her and grabbed her arm, looked to Eli for help and the two helped Harriet to her cabin. Eli told her, "I'll do everything I can to get them back, you try not to worry. I know you'll pray and that's what it'll take."

He returned to the salon where Twofer waited, "So, how we gonna do this swap? Did he say?" asked Eli.

"He said he'd flag us down or sumpin' so keep a lookout!" answered Twofer.

"He's probably going to the Sioux to get some help," suggested Eli. He shook his head as he looked around, "We can't let the Sioux get those rifles..." he mumbled.

He looked to Twofer, "I'm goin' to talk to the captain, maybe come up with an idea or something."

"I'm comin' with!" declared Twofer as Eli started to the door to take the stairs to the Texas deck.

————

THE RISING sun was chasing the boat upstream on the Big Muddy when the captain led Eli from the pilothouse, having turned over the wheel to the pilot, Barnaby Nichols. As they stepped to the rail, "It'll be risky, but I don't see any other way. We need wood since we couldn't get any back at the last woodyard. So, it's only natural we stop to cut some for ourselves, and when we do, then you and Twofer and whoever else you can get to help, can…" and he detailed his plan to replace the rifles with rocks, giving weight to the boxes, and more.

"We'll have to keep a close watch for the Sioux, they might be following and watching," suggested Eli.

"Well, we'll stop on the north bank, that'll help, but we'll need to be quick about it and have some standin' guard just in case. If we can pull it off, I think it'll work."

Eli looked at Twofer who nodded his agreement and then to the captain, "We'll get busy doin' our part. Hopefully we'll get it done 'fore we stop."

"You've got 'tween an hour an' two," answered the captain.

————

THE BRASS SHIP'S lantern sat on a box marked *Picks, Shovels, and Pans* bound for the Helena Miner's Supply. Eli used the crowbar to pry the lids off the boxes and Twofer dug in to pull out the Sharps carbines. They stacked the rifles between the hull and the row of bundled cargo and left the boxes open and lined out. The Bibles and other books were stacked at the ends of each of the boxes, ready to cover the new contents. The two men crawled from under the hatch cover, dirty, sweaty, and anxious for some fresh air and hot coffee.

The captain was standing in the prow, waiting for them, and said, "Just in time. We're about to make that stop for wood," pointing to the nearing north shore. It was the mouth of a small inlet, and abundant with trees. "We've got a couple rock sleds we used to bring the wood on board. You can use one to bring the *ballast* aboard." He cocked his head to the side so Eli would understand what he was to say about the rocks. "Since we'll be offloading some cargo, we'll need the ballast to keep things upright, you understand."

"I understand, Captain. We're glad to help."

Part of the price for the low-cost tickets for passengers on the main deck, was the requirement for the men to help whenever the boat had to stop and cut wood. As the boat nosed into the bank, the mate went among the passengers, rounding up the men to help with the gather. Eli grabbed a couple husky-looking men that appeared to be no strangers to hard work, and with Twofer at his side, they dragged one of the skids down the ramp and went to the edge of the bluff where a big rock outcropping promised all they needed.

It took four skid loads of rocks to provide the necessary 'ballast' as required by the captain, and as soon as the rocks were lowered into the hold, the men were dismissed to join the wood cutters. Eli and Twofer used a box lid to drag the rocks to where they were needed and worked feverishly to fill the emptied boxes, cover the rocks with a layer of books and Bibles just like they had been packed before, and reseal the lids. They were almost finished when they felt the boat begin to pull back from the shore and turn into the current. When they came from the hold, the fresh air was savored as they stood at the rail near the prow.

It was approaching midday when Eli, standing at the rail on the Texas deck, spotted the man standing on the broad sandbar and motioning for them to stop. He used his field glasses to be certain it was one of the gunrunners, and recognizing him, turned back to nod at the captain standing in the pilothouse. The captain returned the nod, reached for the bell ropes, and signaled the engine room. Twofer was beside Eli and asked, "You think them fellas will do as you tol' 'em?"

"Hope so, I'm countin' on 'em."

As the big boat nosed into the sandy bank, Eli called out to the man below, "Where's the two captives?"

"We got 'em, an' you need to give o'er them boxes!"

"Nothing is leaving this boat 'til we see those two and see they've not been harmed!"

The man turned and motioned to the edge of the trees and the second of the outlaws, the one known as Bert, pushed Ben and Maribel, hands tied before them and gags over their mouths, into the open. He told them to stop, and made them stand before him, shielding him from any shooters. The man closer to the shore, Skip Martin, hollered up, "There they are! Now, let's have them cargo boxes!"

Eli lifted his rifle and answered the man below, "You back away, nobody is touching those boxes until they're all offloaded, and the captives are at the foot of this ramp."

"How will we know the rifles are in the boxes?"

"When the last box is stacked, one of our men will open one and show you!"

Eli could hear the man grumble, and he watched as Skip Martin moved away to stand further up on the shore but stayed close enough to watch the unloading. Eli leaned over the rail and spoke to the mate, who was waiting at the hatch cover, and said, "Alright, Hunter, start with the boxes."

The engine below continued to hiss and huff as the steam whistled from the overflow valve, and the men hustled along as they dragged the boxes from the hold and lifted them over the hatch to hand off to those that would carry the cargo, two men to a box. It was but a short while when the last of the six boxes was walked down the gangplank, followed by the mate. He directed the others to stack the box on top, dismissed them and with crowbar in hand, pried open the lid. Skip Martin started forward, but Eli fired a warning round at his feet, "Stay back!"

The mate made a show of prying open the lid, rummaging past the books, and withdrew a rifle. He held it overhead, as he faced the trees, then replaced it in the box, the lid sitting off to the side. The mate turned away and started for the gangplank as Eli called, "Alright, bring the captives down!"

Skip Martin growled, but motioned to his partner and Bert started forward, nudging Ben with the muzzle of his rifle. Bert stopped beside Skip and told the two captives to keep walking. Ben quietly spoke to Maribel, "When we get to the gangplank, don't waste any time going up the plank, I reckon Eli's got something planned."

Eli watched the two young people come closer, spoke softly to Twofer, "Get ready." Twofer answered, "Been ready. Git them kids aboard!"

As the two approached the gangplank, Skip watched and turned, cupped his hands to his mouth and shouted, "Now!" As Eli suspected, several warriors came screaming from the trees, firing at the boat, and charging forward. With a glance to the plank, Eli saw Ben and Maribel hit the deck and he hollered to the captain, "Move now!"

He waited until Skip and Bert were near the boxes and several of the warriors gathered around and both Eli and Twofer fired. Their target was a black *X* marked on the bottom box about in the middle. Their bullets hit the target almost simultaneously and the boxes exploded. Wood, books, and rocks flew in every direction, taking everything and everyone nearby down as the explosion erupted like an ancient volcano, spewing death and dealing bits all about. Eli and Twofer had packed all the ammunition together in the middle of the bottom box, marked the box, and used that as their target. When the ammunition exploded, the lead bullets of the paper cartridges flew indiscriminately and dealt death all around.

The boat had already pulled back from the shore and the paddle wheel was churning the water, driving the boat into the current and away from the shore. Arrows rattled against the rail, fell into the water, until the boat was totally out of range of any of the survivors' arrows. Eli looked back as the dark grey and black smoke drifted away revealing many bodies—powder burned beyond recognition—scattered about the upper bank. He shook his head at the unnecessary deaths, "That's a mighty high price to pay for the greed of a handful."

"Ummhmm. But I'm mighty glad they got the bill and not us!" answered Twofer.

CHAPTER 28

MANDAN

As the big boat chugged away, leaving the usual pale froth in its wake, the remaining warriors moved about the dead and wounded. As they neared the center of the blast, Kicking Bear was startled when one of the bodies moved, rolling to the side. He jumped back, lowering his lance toward the movement when Skip Martin growled and grumbled as he rolled from under the body of his partner. He looked up at Kicking Bear, "What'd you say?" he was hollering, and the Indian looked at him, wide-eyed, and began chanting.

Martin pushed the body of his partner away, rolled to his hands and knees and struggled to stand. He looked around, put his hands to his ringing ears, and shook his head. He turned to look at the disappearing boat as it rounded the bend, paddle wheel churning in the water. He growled, "I'm gonna get that..." shaking his fist at the retreating boat. He looked at Kicking Bear, "What're you lookin' at? Ain't you never seen somebody come back from the dead?"

"Aiiieee," shouted the warrior, backstepping away

from the dirty white man. He looked at the remaining warriors and shouted at them, motioning to the trees and the bunch of them went to the trees for their horses. As Kicking Bear passed the bodies of his fellow warriors, Black Elk and Red Horse, he shook his lance at them and muttered a chant, and quickly followed the others. As they took to the horses, the looks from the others asked the obvious, and Kicking Bear ordered, "Go, get the bodies, we will take them to the village and let the shaman tend to them."

Skip Martin watched the Sioux gather the bodies of their fellow warriors, counting himself lucky to be alive, knowing Kicking Bear could have easily killed him because he failed to deliver the rifles as promised. But he could tell by the debris that littered the area that the rifles were not in the boxes and must still be aboard the boat, and that meant he could still finagle a way to get them and deliver them to Red Cloud as originally planned.

———————

"MA!" pleaded Ben as his mother held him tight, sobbing against his chest.

"Don't you 'Ma' me! I thought I had lost you and it scared me to death!" she replied, refusing to let him go as she looked up at him. "You may think you're a man, but you're still my little boy!"

Ben chuckled as his little sisters joined in the hug. Nora and Millie wrapped their arms around his waist, one on either side and agreed with their Ma, "That's right," declared the older Nora, "you're still our brother!"

Ben returned the hugs and said, "I'll always be your

brother and your son, Ma, but you can let go 'fore you squeeze the life outta me, please!"

Millie stepped back and asked, "Did'ju see the Injuns?"

"Yup, we saw the whole war party."

"Did they scalp you?" she asked, looking up at his hair.

Ben bent down so his sister could see, "No! See, I still have all my hair!"

Both girls looked closely, and Nora said, "Ewhhh, don't you ever wash it? It looks like bugs live there!"

"Alright, you two. Let your brother be, I reckon he needs to get some rest or something," suggested Harriet, looking with pride at her boy.

"Something? You mean like seeing Maribel?" giggled Nora, smiling at Ben.

"Maybe, but I was thinking about getting me a cup of coffee first," grinned Ben, trying to sound very grown-up, but failing to keep a straight face. "Would you like to join me?" he asked, looking at his mother with but a glance to the girls.

"Why yes, *Mr.* Hamilton, I think we would like to have some refreshment with you," answered a smiling Harriet as she slipped her hand under his arm.

———

THE NEXT STOP was a brief one at Fort Sully. They needed to top off their stacks of wood and Eli took advantage of the stop to report to the commandant about the attacks and the gunrunners. He was ushered into the commandant's office and the man behind the desk, Lieutenant Colonel John Pattee, stood and extended his hand, "Colonel McCain, is it?"

"Formerly, yes. But now it's just Elijah McCain." He shook the commandant's hand and was seated. "I just wanted to give you a report that you might be interested in, Colonel." Eli related the happenings regarding the shipment of rifles, the gunrunners, the attacks by the Sioux, and the last conflict. "So, Colonel, now we have about a hundred twenty Sharps carbines that we would like to keep out of the hands of the Natives. Any ideas?"

The colonel chuckled, "That is an unusual problem. But the 7th Iowa Cavalry, the unit stationed here for now, is equipped with the Spencer repeaters and have no need for the Sharps. But," he paused, leaned forward on the desk, "they're building a Fort Buford at the mouth of the Yellowstone, and that outfit was kind of low down the line as far as new equipment. They might like to get the Sharps."

"That sounds like a good solution, as long as we don't get attacked again and have 'em taken from us, but..." Eli shrugged and stood, extending his hand to shake and the colonel offered, "I'll have a company of cavalry follow along as you leave, just to make our presence known and if there's any of the same bunch following, that'll probably discourage them."

"Thanks, Colonel, that'll make Captain Marsh feel better." They shook and Eli turned to leave, departed the fort, and returned to the boat. He relayed the colonel's offer, and the captain did indeed feel better about having the armed escort, if for but a short distance.

———

THE MOON WAS WAXING to half and the captain chose to keep moving, making up for lost time. The boat traveled through the quiet of the night, leaving behind the smell of wood smoke and the churned-up waters. They were not the only boat on the river and often passed others going downstream, loaded with pelts, miners, and gold, and bound for St. Louis. After leaving Fort Sully, the journey was almost boring, with the usual stops for wood and occasionally delivering and loading cargo. They were still in Sioux territory and often saw parties of warriors but suffered no more attacks. A week of constant travel brought them to the mouth of the Heart River, and the captain pointed out, "That there," pointing to the mouth of the Heart, "is the northern boundary of the Sioux territory, not that they pay much attention to it. But that's what they all agreed on at the Treaty of Fort Laramie of 1851. Just beyond there is the land of the Arikara, Mandan, and Gros Ventre. But their land ain't as big as the land of the Sioux."

"So, we're over halfway to Fort Benton?"

"Yup, but this half can be more hazardous, what with sandbars, snags, sweepers, and such. Not as much water in these upper reaches so we won't be doin' as much night travel, except when the moon's full, then maybe..." he shrugged, lifting his cup of coffee for a sip. He was leaning against the side wall of the pilothouse, adding his eyes to those of the pilot who was at the wheel.

———

BY MIDMORNING the captain had taken his turn at the wheel and he and Eli stood at the rail overlooking the prow of the boat. He frowned and lifted his hand to point, "Looks like some Natives want to do some trading. Probably Mandan, good people and good traders. That's Like-a-Fishhook Village, there's Mandan, Arikara, and Hidatsa all living there. They're some of the few

Natives that raise most of their own food and when they trade, they usually have corn, squash, and more. And that's Fort Berthold over yonder," nodding toward the stockade structure. "Course, this early in the season, anything the Mandan and Hidatsa have will be dried but it's still good."

The captain had already told the pilot to go to the shore and the boat nosed into the sandy bank as two men jumped from the prow, ropes in hand to tie off the boat while the trades took place. The village stood above the river on the higher bank. Large dome shaped earthen lodges were uniformly scattered about, the doorways facing the east and a central compound where many of the celebrations and more occurred. Several of the people were walking down the bank, goods in hand, ready to make trade with those on the boat. Eli came from his cabin, a parfleche hanging from his shoulder as he spotted Constance Wellington. She saw his parfleche, "So, are you going ashore among those Natives to do some trading?"

"Yes, I am. There's a few things that I'd like to trade for, if they have what I'd like. Would you like to join me?"

She smiled, nodded, "Yes, I would. I've never had the opportunity to see the trades and I think it would be quite interesting."

ELI FOUND a spot among the traders and spread out a blanket and began arranging his goods for display. Constance sat down on a rock and watched as Eli dug into his parfleche. She did not recognize all that he brought out but watched as several of the Natives, women and men alike, stopped and watched. He spread out several small mirrors, some buttons, some blue-and-white beads, some needles, a half dozen combs, several knives, and some vermillion and verdigris. He sat back and watched as some women, timid at first, began to finger the goods and asked, using sign language and some broken English, about what the different items would take to trade.

He responded in English and sign that he learned when stationed at Fort Laramie and began to bicker. When he reached an agreement, they shook hands, and the women went to get the goods agreed upon. He sat back, looked at Constance, "What do you think?"

"Interesting. So, what did you trade for?"

He chuckled, "Well, depends on what it really is, but I was asking for moccasins, and a buckskin jacket. I agreed to take some corn, and some jewelry. We'll see what it is when they return."

The captain passed among the traders, telling those from the boat to get aboard, the boat would be leaving soon. After he passed, the women returned, and Eli was happy with everything. The high-topped moccasins were a perfect fit as was the long buckskin jacket. The jewelry was made with silver and had a couple small gold nuggets which he considered a bonus and gave more than he agreed. But everyone went away happy and satisfied and Eli and Constance returned to the boat. As they stepped aboard, Eli handed Constance the silver bracelet with the single gold nugget and said, "That's for you. A little memento of the trip."

"Eli! This is beautiful! Thank you!" she replied, slipping the bracelet on her wrist, and admiring the workmanship. She looked at Eli and moved closer, lifted up on tiptoes and planted a kiss on his lips.

"Whooooaa, I didn't expect that!" he declared, smiling, and starting up the steps to the salon.

"You've done so much for everyone, thank you!" answered Constance, admiring her bracelet as they climbed the stairs.

Eli lifted eyebrows as he thought of the kiss. It had been a long time since he had any attention from a woman or wanted to give any attention to a woman. Maybe things were changing.

CHAPTER 29

FORT BUFORD

Three days out of Fort Berthold and the Mandan village, they approached the mouth of the Little Missouri River that flowed in from the south. The captain's plan was to stop for some wood as the usual wood hawks were commonly found there, but they met with a scene of devastation. The remains of the pilothouse of the riverboat, *Lilly Peck*, protruded askew from the water. Where the hull, decks, and cabins should be, water rippled past as if there had never been an obstruction. At water's edge, burnt and split boards yielded to the current that pushed the debris to the sandy shore. Pieces of metal, probably from exploded boilers and more, were strewn along the bank. One big tree wore a badge of black metal protruding from its lower trunk, but the wounds of split limbs showed raw, with withered branches gathered at the foot of the once proud cottonwood. Five people stood, waving and holding on to one another, surrounded by debris from the once proud riverboat.

The captain motioned for the pilot to pull into shore

and as the boat nosed into the sandy embankment, the gangplank was lowered and the five people limped toward the long plank. Several of the passengers had come to the port side of the *Louella* to gawk at the remains of the riverboat and the surviving passengers. Eli stood beside the captain as the survivors shuffled up the plank and onto the deck. Marsh stepped forward, "Welcome aboard, folks. I'm Captain Marsh."

The apparent leader of the small group was a man with a bandaged arm, but he extended his hand to shake with the captain, "Thank you, Captain. I must say, you are a sight for sore eyes! We were beginning to wonder if ours was the only boat on the river and were about to give up hope. Thanks so much for stopping, you've certainly saved us. Oh, let me introduce you," he turned back toward the others. "I am Eustis Reynolds, and this is Lillian Crabtree, her husband was killed in the explosion. These are Gerald Lucy, Fred Weisel, and Jerome Monahan. The four of us," motioning to the other men, "are headed to the goldfields. Originally, I was going to Last Chance to put in a mercantile, but..." he motioned to the debris, "that was the end of my shipment of goods."

Eli stepped forward, "Let me add my welcome to the captain's. I'm Elijah McCain," and extended his hand to shake with the men, tipped his hat to the woman, and turned to the captain. "Should we get these folks to the salon, tend to their injuries, and maybe make up the empty cabins for them?"

"Certainly," answered the captain. "If you would be so kind as to lead the way?" and motioned Eli to the stairs and the salon.

Eli nodded, motioned to the others to follow, and started up the stairs. He spoke over his shoulder to the woman, "I'm certain you find yourself without your outfit, but we have several fine ladies aboard that I believe will be happy to lend a hand to a lady in distress."

"That would be wonderful, Mr. McCain, thank you."

As he topped the steps, he saw Constance and Harriet at the rail, doing as the others and looking at the site of the explosion and resulting damage. They turned when they heard Eli, and he asked, "Ladies, this is Lillian Crabtree, she lost her husband in the wreck of the *Lilly Peck* and could use some help. Would you be so kind as to see to the injuries of all of our new passengers and maybe help Mrs. Crabtree with some necessities?"

"Of course, Eli," answered Harriet, showing an expression of compassion as she stepped forward and offered her hand to assist the woman. But Constance was not as quick to offer, looking from Eli to Lillian and back to Eli again, her eyes flashing a little doubt, but relaxed and followed the others, turning away from Eli as she passed.

Eli chuckled to himself, shaking his head, and thinking, *women!* Eli returned to the bow of the boat where the captain was talking with the mate. The captain saw Eli approaching and dismissed the mate, turned to Eli, and said, "We were going to get wood here, but as you can see it appears all the trees have been cut and the Woodhawks moved on, so, we'll keep going and hope to find them sooner than later."

The river had turned westerly, and the water was growing more shallow, and the banks drew nearer. Where in the lower reaches, the river was a half-mile wide and sometimes more, now it was commonly less than a thousand feet between the banks. Fortunately, the next woodyard was about seven miles upstream and a large stack of wood showed beside a flag waving in the wind. A young man, Native, stood near the pile and motioned for the boat to stop. The captain, standing at the rail on the Texas deck beside Eli, frowned, and without taking his eyes off the woodpile and the young man, spoke to Eli, "You might want to get your rifle, just in case."

Eli quickly took the stairs down to the cabin deck, retrieved his rifle, and returned to the captain's side just as the boat nosed into the bank and began lowering the gangplank. The young man nodded, started down the bank and shouted up to the captain, "I am Stands Back of the Gros Ventre people. The men are cutting more wood and I will make the deal. They will return shortly."

The captain looked at Eli and back to the young man and nodded. "I'll be right down!"

The captain and the young man had made the deal and before his crew could get to the shore, several Native men were already loading a horse-drawn sled with wood and preparing to bring it to the boat. When the crew worked together with the Natives, the wood was quickly aboard, and the deal concluded. As the captain paid off in supplies and coin, he shook hands and the boat backed away, lifting the plank as it moved. The captain looked at Eli, "That was one of the best deals for wood for this entire trip. Good wood, good price, and they helped load it." He grinned, shaking his head as he took to the stairs to return to his quarters behind the pilothouse.

——————

IT WAS MIDMORNING on the third day after the Gros Ventre sold them wood, that the *Louella* approached the mouth of the Yellowstone River. They pushed past the

Yellowstone, the Missouri making a deep bend south and back to the north. As the river started to bend to the west, the boat nosed into the bank just below an encampment of soldiers amid evidence of the construction of a new fort. "That'd be the Fort Buford the commandant at Fort Sully mentioned. It's a new one alright and it appears they have their work cut out for 'em," declared Captain Marsh. "I'll let you go talk to the soldiers 'bout those rifles. In the meantime, we'll sit and enjoy some coffee while you're gone. It doesn't look like the soldiers would be too happy if we were to go cuttin' any of their trees," chuckled the captain.

"And from the look of those fellas, looks like we won't have to wait very long," said Eli, nodding to a handful of soldiers coming down the slight bluff toward the boat. Eli glanced at the captain, shook his head as he chuckled, and started for the gangplank that just touched down. He started down the plank, stopped as the soldiers approached, and noticed the man in the lead was uniformed as an officer; as he neared, he saw the silver oak leaves on his shoulders. "Mornin' Colonel. Good to see you men coming down to welcome us."

Eli grinned as he stepped off the plank and approached the uniformed men, his hand outstretched to shake. The officer nodded, shook Eli's hand, and asked, "Just what are you looking for that you stopped here?"

Eli grinned, "I have something you might be able to put to use. Colonel John Pattee at Fort Sully thought you might could use some Sharps carbines we have aboard."

"You have Sharps? And what would you be doing with Sharps rifles?" asked the Colonel, frowning and showing a touch of suspicion.

Eli explained about the discovery, the gunrunners and the ensuing attack from the Sioux, and the final outcome that left them with the rifles still aboard. "So, you see, Colonel, they're yours if you'll just take 'em off our hands. There is a box of paper cartridges as well, didn't discover that until after the last set-to with the Indians, but they're yours also."

"How many rifles are there?" asked the Colonel.

"I think there's about a hundred twenty."

The colonel's eyes flared, and his forehead wrinkled as hope showed in his countenance. He chuckled, "Friend, you are an answer to prayer! We've already had a couple of attacks by Sitting Bull and his Hunkpapa Lakota. They're doing all they can to discourage the building of this fort, but we're just as determined to get the job completed. We have a total of ninety men in Company C, 2nd Battalion, 13th Infantry, and we've been given orders to get this fort built to protect the river traffic, settlers, gold hunters, and to try to keep peace among the tribes." He sighed heavily, shaking his head, "And so far, it has been a challenge! But these rifles will definitely be a help. All we have currently are the Springfield rifles left over from the war, although I've requested some new Spencers, they're slow in getting anything to us. We were hopeful when we saw your boat, that they might have got some off to us, but the Sharps will be a big help."

———

THE *Louella* WAS SOON on its way again, passed the trading post, Fort Union, and continued up the Big Muddy even after the moon, now waxing past half, lit the way on the clear night. Eli had joined the captain in the pilothouse and listened as the captain explained, "All that you see off the port side is now part of the Assiniboine territory, at least according to the treaty of '51." He chuckled, "Assiniboine means stone Sioux, they say that comes from their practice of using stones in their cooking."

"That's what I learned when I was at Fort Laramie, it seems they heat stones and drop them into water to boil it and cook their meat. Seems practical," added Eli. "But their reputation among those at Laramie were that the Assiniboine were peaceable, at least compared to the other Sioux." Eli looked at the moonlight bouncing off the rippling waters, glanced up at the moon, and turned to the captain, "You expect any problems in the next stretch?"

"No, we've got about a week to go to get to the rougher part of the river. It's a place called Dauphin Rapids and that might give us some challenges, just depends on what the spring melt has done to the river. So far, it appears to be about normal, but..." he shrugged.

CHAPTER 30

COW ISLAND

They had been on the river for seven weeks and most were travel weary. Although the changing landscape offered some variety to the days, the warm weather and gusty winds dimmed anyone's enthusiasm for standing at the rail and watching the sometimes-treeless terrain pass by, the grass and sagebrush waving in the breeze. Constance looked at Eli, smiled, "So, we're getting near our destination, what are your plans?"

Eli grinned, dropped his eyes, and started to explain, "I promised Harriet and her children, and Luther and his family, that I'd see they get to Fort Benton. But they also need to make it to Helena, so I reckon I'll at least see to it that they're on their way, maybe with a wagon and team or on the stage or..." he shrugged. "Now that Luther is getting better, that's good, but he's still not up to handling a team. Of course, Ben is becoming quite capable and he's shining up to Maribel, so maybe."

"But, what about you?"

"I made a promise to my wife that I'd find the twins

and get 'em home. But she has passed, so the getting them home part is not an issue but finding them is still part of that promise. Her concern was for her boys. I wasn't home much while they were growing so they kind of had their way without a lot of correction, and it showed. They did enlist in the Union Army but deserted and ran off without talking to their mother. So, when I got out and went home, she pleaded with me to find them and bring them home. She passed from consumption shortly after and I left to fulfill the covenant I made with her."

"I can't imagine how that must make you feel to not know about your sons and all."

"They're my stepsons, but I'm the only father, although absent most of the time, that they knew. Their father was my friend, but he was killed before the boys were born, and as a promise to him, I married his wife and..." he left the thought hanging between them. After a moment of silence, he grinned at Constance, "I haven't told anyone that entire story, ever."

Constance smiled, touched his arm, and said, "You can always confide in me, Eli, no matter what."

"You're a good friend, Constance. But...I can't make any promises. I don't know where this search is going to take me nor how long."

"I understand. And I have my business to tend to as well. But we can keep in touch and see what happens." She paused as she looked from Eli to the changing terrain, and said wistfully, "I like you, Eli, more than I've ever liked any man since my husband was killed. I would like to see more of you."

Eli chuckled, shaking his head, "I'm afraid that I'd not be much of a bargain for you."

Before they could finish their conversation, the

captain approached, "Good morning, folks. Are you enjoying this nice day I ordered up special?" he wore a broad grin as he neared, for he was always known to be very congenial with all the passengers, but especially to those he had formed a bit of a friendship with like these two.

Constance was the first to reply, "Why thank you, Captain. That's very considerate of you to order up such a special day just for us."

The captain chuckled, "Well, don't get too used to it, we're coming into the stretch of water that's going to be quite the challenge."

"Oh, and what lies ahead that could be worse than what we've already dealt with?" asked Eli, showing a bit of skepticism in his expression.

"Well, I don't think we'll need to worry about Indians, if that's what you're thinking. But we have some shoals, rapids, and more coming up in the next few miles and it might take a little to get past them." He nodded upriver, "There on the starboard side is Grand Island. A few miles further and we'll make a stop at Cow Island, that's where the wagons that take some cargo and portage the rapids or take it on to Fort Benton or other places. When the water is low, many boats offload their cargo here and turn back. But some are able to make it. I think we might have to work at it, but I believe we can make it."

"And what is it when you say you 'might have to work at it'?" queried Constance.

The captain smiled, "It would be easier for you to wait and see than for me to try to explain. Just let me say it's called 'grasshoppering.'" He chuckled at her expression and added, "You'll see, you'll see," and took to the stairs to go to the Texas deck and the pilothouse.

———

To the usual flatlander, the terrain that sandwiched the river was mountainous, with rugged terrain that rose five to seven hundred feet above river level. But to those of this land, these were hills— rugged, yes—but hills and buttes, not mountains. Piñon, cedar, juniper, and buckbrush were sprinkled on the upper reaches and deep ravines of the hills. Gullies, ravines, and arroyos clawed at the hills, leaving scars of previous storms and cataclysms that lent the appearance of giant claws stretching out toward the waterway. The meandering Missouri River wound its way among these monuments to the power of nature and the creative work of God, leaving green flats where the course of water had been, enticing the many animals of the plains to come and graze and take their water. The river made a looping bend to the north around a rugged peninsula of buttes, turning back to the east and then to the northwest before the shoulders of the hill pushed back to show a wide alluvial plain on the west edge of the water, and two courses of the river that held Cow Island captive, keeping the trees and greenery preserved and identifying the landmark for the waterborne travelers.

Two boats were moored on the sandy shore to the east, and Eli could feel the move of the boat as it turned from the current and pointed toward the shoreline. The *William J. Lewis* and the *Leoni Leoti* were tied off to a deadman on shore and cargo was being offloaded from the *William J. Lewis*. The captain came to Eli's side and said, "Remember when I told you that those two that fit the description of your boys had taken to a freighter and left the river?"

"Ummhmm," responded Eli, cocking one eyebrow up as he waited for the captain to explain.

"This is where they left. You might go over there," pointing to several wagons that were lined out near some tents, "and ask around. The mate remembered the freighter they went with was Paquette's." He looked about, turned back to Eli, "We'll be here a while, have to wait our turn takin' to the rapids. Although the rapids are about twenty miles upriver, this is the best place to moor up and wait. We will also take stock of our wood, make sure we have enough to make it to the next wood hawk, but not so much as to weigh us down." He glanced to Eli, "Go ahead, we won't leave without you."

Eli nodded to the captain, tipped his hat to Constance, "Excuse me, ma'am, Captain," and went to his cabin. He did not always carry his weapons with him while on board but was not about to go ashore unarmed. He strapped on his Colt .44 Army pistol, slipped the Bowie knife and scabbard into his waistband at his back and looked at the LeMat pistol and thought about it, lifted it, and checked the loads and slipped it behind his belt at his back, accessible with his left hand, but not readily visible under the tail of the jacket he wore. It was the beaded and fringed buckskin jacket he had traded from the Mandan women and was both warm and comfortable.

Eli started toward the gangplank and saw a freight wagon coming close, two men up top, and drawn by a six-up of mules. The wagon stopped and the two men climbed down and started toward the boat. Eli stood at the prow of the boat near the gangplank and the captain came to his side, "Those two are probably looking for some freight, but we don't have any marked for here, but we'll see what they want."

The two men, both a mite scruffy looking but that was to be expected of teamsters that were not known for their winsome ways, strode up the gangplank, looked to the two men that appeared to be waiting and one called out, "Hey! You the cap'n?"

Marsh stepped forward, "That's right. What do you need?"

"We need some boxes o' cargo. Here's the papers!" he called as he came near the captain and held out a sheath of papers.

The captain accepted the offered papers, looked it over, glanced to Eli, "This is for six boxes of books and Bibles marked for the Blackfoot Mission, care of Fort Benton." He looked up at the two men, "And just what do you have to do with the mission?"

"Uh, nuthin', we was just given them papers, and tol' to come get the boxes." The man in the forefront of the two was the speaker and being downwind of him told both the captain and Eli this man had not been any closer to water than he was at this moment.

The captain coughed, stepped back a little and looked at the two men who appeared just the opposite of one another, the talker was sloppy with his ponderous belly showing between his shirt and britches and his bald pate showing at the edge of his floppy felt hat. The second of the two was tall, lean, and seemingly disjointed as he moved, but he was just as ripe as his partner. The captain looked from one to the other, "I'm afraid you're going to be disappointed. Those boxes are no longer aboard. You see, there was an explosion and those boxes and the contents were blown to smithereens."

Eli stepped forward, frowning, and asked, "Who sent you for those boxes?"

"Our boss, Winifred Paquette, he's the one what owns this comp'ny," answered the first man.

"And you are?" asked Eli.

"Uh, I'm Pug Witcher, and this hyar's Whittaker! But what do that matter who we be?"

"Oh, just wondering," drawled Eli, stepping back with a nod to the captain. But before the captain could speak, Eli turned and asked, "Oh, say, have you men ever met a couple younger men that looked a lot alike, name of Joshua and Jubal Paine?"

Pug looked at Whittaker and back to Eli, "Uh yeah, why?"

"They're friends of mine," replied Eli. "How do you know them?"

"They was freightin' with us, but they done left to go to the goldfield. Said they was gonna work fer some guy what had him a good claim."

"How long ago did they leave?" asked Eli.

"Right 'fore we stayed here. They was takin' a load back to Fort Benton, then they was gonna quit an' go to the goldfield down by Last Chance."

Eli grinned, glanced to the captain, and said, "Guess I'm on the right track!"

The two freighters looked from one to the other and Pug asked, "So, if'n you ain't got 'em, guess we can't haul 'em," and reached for the papers held by the captain. But Captain Marsh said, "No, I'll just keep these, that way I can explain to the Mission what happened to the cargo."

"Oh," responded Pug. He looked from the captain to his friend and nodded down the plank, "We best git."

After the freighters left, the captain and mate dickered with the wood hawks and took on ten cord of wood and were soon ready to try the rapids, but they had to wait a short while as the *Leoni Leoti* pulled away and started up the river. "We'll give 'em about an hour, then we'll follow. They should be past the shoals by the time we get there," stated the captain. He looked at Eli, "Glad you got word of your boys. Do you want to leave from here, or are you going to wait till we get to the fort?"

"I have obligations to the two families I came aboard with, so I'll wait till we get to the fort. Besides, I'd like to find out more about the Blackfoot Mission that ordered those rifles," declared Eli, grinning at the captain.

CHAPTER 31

DAUPHIN RAPIDS

As the *Louella* pushed into the current to take to the main channel and pass Cow Island, the rub of the hull on sandbar shoals told of the force of the current and the movement of the boat over the accumulated sand pushed down from the higher levels by the spring snowmelt. They could feel the bottom as the boat slid over the shoal, scraping the length of the hull. The captain stood beside the pilot as Barnaby Nichols spun the wheel, always cautious of each movement and pull and push of the strong current. Captain Marsh searched the waters for any sign or impediment that could hinder their progress but was relieved when he saw the water was of sufficient depth for their passage.

Shortly after leaving Cow Island, the big shoulders of the hills pushed in, crowding the Big Muddy into a narrower passage. Where before, the river flowed freely along a thousand-foot-wide course, now the steep-sided bluffs stood like sentinels over the seven-hundred-foot-wide channel. Sandy shores that had built up over eons of time and deeper waters from massive snowfalls in the high country, fanned out from the bases of the bluffs, offering scant flats for any vegetation. The fringe of green at the bottom of cliff faces appeared like the collars of fancy dans strutting down the boulevard of wilderness.

The usual meandering river was held to its more direct course by unrelenting hills and bluffs, and the narrow channel flowed deeper, much to the advantage of the early spring travelers. Deep coulees held their mystery close between the buttes and steep-walled arroyos let the wind whistle like long dead banshees. The warning from the captain of rough waters ahead merely added to the tension felt among crew and passengers alike, but that apprehension blossomed into outright fear when the boat nosed over another sandy shoal and the lookout shouted, "There! The rapids, dead ahead! Looks to be a boat in the middle of 'em!"

The *Louella* had just cleared a slight bend to the southwest and the river pointed due west. Just over a half mile before them, the gurgling water of the Dauphin Rapids showed themselves as the formidable obstacle that gave the passage its feared reputation. The stern of the *Leoni Leoti* could be seen as the long spars stood before its prow. The captain took the wheel from the pilot and grabbed the bell ropes to signal the engine room for more steam. With a glance to the pilot, "Here's hopin' the *Leoni* will crest those rapids 'fore we hit them. I wanna have our steam up and making as much headway as possible 'fore we get there."

Barnaby Nichols nodded to the captain, fully aware of challenging rapids, and understanding the captain's tactic to get as far into and up the rapids as possible before the boat ground ashore on the rocky bottom. He only hoped that the strong assault would not damage the hull for it was easy for the jagged stones that formed the rapids to tear long gashes into the hull and bring their assault to a quick end. Nichols lifted the binoculars, "Looks like they're draggin' in the spars, the wheel's churnin' and they're movin'! They'll be clear of the rapids 'fore we hit 'em, Captain!"

At the sounding of the alarm by the lookout, passengers and crew crowded the rails, leaning forward as if their view of the river would be improved by the few inches of their lean. But people are always prone to allow their bodily movements to reveal their own tensions and fears as well as curiosities. Eli stood at the rail beside Constance and Harriet, shading his eyes from the afternoon glare that bounced off the water and danced on the ripples. The chug, chug, chug of the steam engines driving the long pitman shaft at the paddle wheel seemed to increase its pace with the eagerness of the riverboat charging at the rapids. The Mate, Hunter Fleming, came forward and began shouting at the passengers, "Get to the stern! Now! Everybody has to move to the back of the boat or go to your cabins! We need the weight off the prow when we hit those rapids!" Mumbles and complaints came from the crowd on both the cabin deck and the main deck, as reluctant passengers trudged away from the unfolding spectacle. Although fearful of what might happen, they wanted to watch. The inimitable draw of the curious minds and the attraction to see the happening of tragedies prompted many to keep looking over their shoulders as they moved away from the rails, reluctant to leave and desirous of being among the few that actually witnessed the coming assault of the rapids.

A single member of the crew stood at the prow, continually taking soundings as he tossed the weighted line into the water, visually marked the point on the line and reeled it in to turn and sound the reading to the pilothouse. He shouted, "five feet plus" and turned to throw the warp again for another reading. As the boat drew closer, the warp showed fifty-two inches.

The pilot looked to the captain, "Fifty-two inches, sir!"

"We're still good," replied the captain, his teeth grinding and jaw muscles flexing. Eyes wide, his grip on the wheel showed white knuckles and his wide stance was firm and unmoving. He kept his eyes on the coming rapids, picking his point of charge, watching the moving of the waters and the splashing of rapids to mentally mark the presence of underwater rocks that pushed the water about. "Here we go!" declared the captain, breathing hard and leaning into the wheel.

The prow of the boat lifted, water splashing over the gunnels, and the boat drove unrelenting into the roaring foam. The rapids looked like stairsteps, each one just a little higher, a little rougher, and each one more powerful and merciless as if fought against the onslaught of the steaming beast that charged into its belly. The hull was growling and grinding as it slid over each obstacle, but the progress of the boat slowed, the engine still chugging and the wheel still pushing, but the big boat finally yielded to the combined power of the current and the clawing of the rocks and the craft stilled in its progress. The foamy water splashed over the gunnels and the roar of the angry rapids continued as the mate shouted orders to extend the spars—big poles, longer than the typical pole used to carry the wires of the telegraph—forward to be lowered to the bottom of the river at a 45-degree angle. Once the poles touched bottom on solid footing, cables that were attached to the bottom of the spars were attached to a rotating capstan, and with the power of the steam engine, they began reeling in the cables. This configuration mimicked the appearance of the rear legs of a grasshopper, and the boat was slowly walked forward by the powerful force of the steam engine-driven winch until the boat touched the spars. Then the big poles were angled out again, planted, and drawn back, walking the boat, or sliding the hull over the rocks and sandy shoals, yard by yard.

The ruckus and noise had drawn the people from their places, and the crowds now leaned at the rails, watching the curious action of the crew and equipment. Constance glanced back at Eli with a grin, "Grasshoppering!" she declared, finally understanding what the captain had said. She looked again, awed by the ingenuity of the simple contraption, and the effectiveness of the work. As the boat neared the crest of the rapids, the prow hung in the air and as the balance of weight pulled, the boat teetered and dropped the prow into the deeper water. But still the spars had to be used, again and again, until the paddle wheel was in deep water and began to lurch against the waves and push the boat forward. With the spars tucked away, the boat seemed to breathe a sigh of relief and renewed its drive against the current.

Several of the passengers had moved to the stern to watch the approach of another stern-wheeler riverboat as it neared the rapids. As it splashed into the rapids, their view was suddenly obscured as the *Louella* took the bend to the south around the point of rocks to continue on its way. The hills had pushed back and the alluvial plain from the south bordered a broad valley that carried a dry creek bed that just weeks earlier carried snowmelt runoff. There were more rapids ahead and the captain, now standing at the rail beside Eli and Constance said, "Those are the Little Dog Rapids, but the water's deep and we won't have any problem with those. They're about the same as Bear Rapids that we passed this side of Cow Island. Now further on there are other rapids and shoals that change all the time, but the bigger of those is Drowned Man Rapids which we'll get to in a few miles. I'm hopin' they'll be passable without havin' to grasshopper."

Constance smiled, looked at the captain, "Now I understand what you mean when you use that expression. You were right, it is easier to understand when you see it. I'm sure I would not have believed you had you tried to explain it before."

The captain grinned, nodded, and with a tip of his cap, "Then you'll excuse me, ladies, Eli?" and walked around the promenade to talk to the other passengers passing out his reassurances like it was tasty candy, and received in the same way. Eli looked at the ladies, "Well, it's mighty close to suppertime. How 'bout we return to the salon and partake of this evening's offerings?"

"Suits me!" declared Constance, slipping her hand through the crook of Eli's arm, and turning to smile at Harriet who agreed with, "Remember when we were children and would race each other to the dinner table?" and laughed.

The laughter and conversation in the salon were a mite more boisterous as the crew served the tables. Smiles were common, and comments exchanged about their new experience of mastering the rapids of the river. Thoughts and emotions were shared as the food was passed and enjoyed. They all knew their long voyage would soon come to an end; they were less than three days out of Fort Benton, and for many that would be their journey's end. Yet others saw this as just a leg of a much longer journey and had some apprehension for the next passage. With most passenger riverboats ending their journey here, many passengers would be continuing their journey by wagon, horseback, or stagecoach, each with its own perils. But for now, relief was the wine that was enjoyed, and laughter prevailed as they dined together once again.

CHAPTER 32

MISSION

The moon was waxing full in the middle of the star-filled night. Moonlight danced on the ripples and the night was quiet as the big paddle-wheeler chugged its way up the Big Muddy. Eli stood with elbows on the rail as he looked at the dimly lit landscape. The hills, though rugged and scarred by the many arroyos and coulees, had retreated away from the water, leaving the rich alluvial plains at river's edge. A herd of elk lifted heads as the boat passed, but soon returned to their moonlight graze undisturbed and undaunted by the steaming beast of the river. The boat had taken a dogleg bend to the south and Eli knew, as the captain had foretold, that they would soon be approaching the mouth of the Marias River, next stop Fort Benton.

Eli's solitude and reverie were interrupted when Chaplain Haney stepped to his side. The chaplain did as Eli, clasped hands, elbows on the rail, and turned to look at Eli. "We haven't talked much, even though the journey has been long."

Eli returned the gaze, looked back to the shadows of the shore, "It has been an interesting passage, has it not?"

"Indeed. More excitement than I was used to, even during the war," answered the chaplain.

Eli glanced at the older man, "You said you were going to start a ministry and maybe an outreach to the local Natives, have you made any decisions as to just what you might do?"

"Well, before I left St. Louis, I was approached by a representative of a mission who asked if I would be willing to become involved with their work, and I expect to meet their people after we dock at Fort Benton. Beyond that, I'm leaning toward going to the new settlement called Helena, in the middle of the goldfields, and try to reach those that have left families and home in search of riches, you know, try to teach them about the true riches to be found in Christ."

"The mission, what is the name?"

"I believe it is just called the Blackfoot Mission," replied the chaplain, frowning as he looked at Eli, suspecting something.

"Did they ask you to do anything for them, you know, take something to the mission for them?"

The chaplain turned to look at Eli, "Why?"

"Just answer, please, it's important."

"They said there would be a shipment on board of Bibles and more, all bound for the mission, but personally, no, they did not ask that I carry anything. They did ask that when the shipment is unloaded, that I try to keep track of it until their people came."

"So, you have no idea what was in the boxes?" queried Eli, facing the man.

"No, other than what they said, Bibles and such, just

supplies for the mission." The chaplain leaned back against the rail post, brow furrowed with curiosity, and added, "But there's something you're not telling me. What is it?"

"Chaplain, because I knew you when, so I'm going to trust you. The 'Blackfoot Mission' might not even exist. The people you spoke with, the ones that put together the shipment of Bibles and such, were nothing but gunrunners, using the name of a mission to cover their shipment of Sharps rifles, bound for the Indians."

"But that can't be, they were sincere and spoke of all the work that had already been done among the Natives. They were hopeful of doing so much more," pleaded the chaplain.

"Probably. But the 'so much more' was not the spreading of the Gospel of Jesus but putting to use what some had called Beecher's Bibles. The six cargo boxes *had* a layer of books and Bibles, but underneath were Sharps rifles and ammunition. But, if you remember when we were attacked by the Sioux, they were after those rifles that they heard were bound for Red Cloud of the Oglala Sioux. And when they had taken the young couple hostage, it was to get those same rifles, but as you might remember, that plan blew up in their faces!"

Eli turned away from the chaplain, resumed his stance at the rail. As he looked at the dim blue light of the moon as it lay on the land, he added, "Those rifles would have killed hundreds of soldiers and settlers, but fortunately they are now in the hands of soldiers at Fort Buford."

"I had no idea," mumbled the chaplain, shaking his head in consternation.

Eli looked back at the man, "If you mean that, maybe you could help. We want to find those that were instrumental in putting that shipment together, but to do that, we need to see who comes to pick them up at the dock. We already had freighters looking for them back when we stopped at Cow Island, but they knew nothing. They were just freighters looking to pick up boxes they were sent for by their boss, the owner of the freight company. If you'll play along, maybe we can find out when they look for the shipment at Fort Benton."

The chaplain slowly nodded, "I'll do whatever I can to help."

――――――

THE SUN WAS GIVING warning of its soon rising as it painted the eastern skies in shades of pink with a dash of orange. The bellies of the few low-lying clouds off their left shoulder blushed crimson and the silhouetted cottonwoods waved their welcome to the new day with fluttering leaves now tinted in an embarrassing color. A solitary Eli, pondering the day ahead, stood at the forward rail, looking at the retreating flattop mesas as they pushed away from the river bottom of the Marias River where it ran to its confluence with the Missouri. He knew they would arrive at the fort sometime after midday, and he still did not know what to expect, nor what he would do when he met those expecting the shipment of rifles.

He was not an officer of the law and no longer an officer of the military. He had no authority, other than the conscious authority of his obligation to do what was right. He remembered the words, or something similar, of the Irish statesman and philosopher, Edmund Burke, who was thought to have said, "All it takes for evil to triumph is for good men to do nothing." He didn't know if those were the right words from the statesman, but that was the way his father had quoted it to him. He remembered his father always encouraging him to take a stand for what he knew was right. He often said, "Concern yourself not with the consequences, just remember that if you fail to stand for what is right, there will be worse consequences suffered by not only yourself, but many others. A man cannot go to his grave with anything so significant on his conscience. You *will* one day stand before God." With a heavy sigh, he turned away from the rail and started back to the salon. He would join his friends for the first meal of the day and talk to them about what to expect when they land.

———

ELI STOOD BESIDE CONSTANCE, watching the terrain change and pass slowly by as the *Louella* continued its onslaught against the current of the Big Muddy. She pointed to the west bank, "Those are not as high as further back, near the rapids." The rising buttes appeared to be shaved off, leaving a wide expanse of flat land of broad plateaus. Behind them, the east bank retained its more rugged appearance with jagged hills made so by the many arroyos, ravines, and coulees.

"There's a lot of land here in the West that some would think of as wasteland, growing nothing but a variety of cacti and lots of Indian grasses and buffalo grass. But they'd be wrong because this wide land supports a wide variety of both plant life and animal life. That mesa there, for example, is probably home to big herds of antelope or pronghorns, deer, coyotes, wolves, foxes, snowshoe rabbits, prairie dogs, and maybe even a few elk as well as black bear. The Natives know how to survive in this land, dependent on the bison or buffalo, and often following the herds, moving their villages behind. It's a wild land, but a beautiful land." He paused as he looked around, "And in the distance there," nodding to the far west, "the Rocky Mountains rise so high you'd swear they were scratching the heavens themselves with granite-tipped peaks that have never been topped by living man. The snowcapped peaks in the wintertime that are framed by a cobalt blue sky are a rare beauty that will take your breath away."

She smiled as she looked at him, "You love this land, don't you?"

He dropped his eyes, chuckled, "Yeah, I suppose I do. It is an amazing country and once you've seen it, walked around it, let it get into your system, it's impossible to get out of your mind."

She pointed to the southwest, "That looks like it's Fort Benton!"

"I believe it is. There's a hotel, the Grand Hotel, that I understand is the best. If you take a room there, I will see you later and perhaps we can have dinner."

"That would be nice. I'll look forward to it," answered Constance, smiling.

———

THREE STEAMERS WERE ALREADY MOORED at the long levee at Fort Benton. The *William J. Lewis* and the *Leoni Leoti* lay side by side, while a little further was the smaller *Bertha*. Captain Marsh steered the *Louella* in between the *Leoni* and the *Bertha*. Nosing into the levee, he cut the engines and let the big boat easily slide into place, the sandbar lifting the prow slightly. He had already told the passengers about disembarking and the unloading of cargo and the planks had barely touched ground when the many passengers, loaded down with their gear, crowded their way to the shore. Constance and Harriet stood side by side at the rail of the promenade walkway, watching the others, and looking about at the bustling and growing town.

The captain had explained the last time he was here the town had fourteen saloons, three hotels, two livery stables, one wagon maker, two trading posts, and three mercantiles. "The way it's been growing, what with the multiple gold strikes, it might be twice that size now. And with the Mullan Road that begins there, Fort Benton has become a hub of roadways and more. Some of the cargo you'll see on the levee will be loaded on the freighters and carried overland to the Columbia River and then on to the west coast."

The levee was busy with freighters loading the cargo from other boats, wagons awaiting some of the prospectors and settlers, other opportunists looking for a mark, and more. A carriage pulled alongside the growing stack of cargo near the *Louella* and Constance waved at the driver. He doffed his hat and stepped down to tether the team to a heavy weight he dropped on the sand. As he started toward the boat, Constance said her goodbyes to Harriet and motioned the driver to come aboard. She stood on the stairs and told him of her baggage and as she made her way to the carriage, the driver fetched her baggage.

Eli had told Harriet and Mildred about the Rialto Hotel and suggested they take a room, and he would meet them for supper, and they would plan the next portion of their trip to Helena.

CHAPTER 33

ACCOUNTS

Eli was on the main deck, saddling his horse and packhorse and loading his gear when Chaplain Haney came into the stall area. "Eli, I noticed a familiar face by the stack of cargo, watching it being unloaded. I don't know if he's with the 'mission' but..." he shrugged.

"Who was it?"

"You remember the four men that always sat together and kept to themselves? I believe they got off some ways back at one of the woodyards or something." He looked at Eli, frowning, "and he's not alone. There is at least one other, maybe two."

Eli slowly nodded, "I remember them, but I thought they were all dead. Two had been killed when the Sioux attacked the boat, and that explosion on shore where the Sioux were should have killed them both."

"I'm certain it's him, the one that seemed to be the leader," added Haney.

"Then wait until I'm ready before you go down there. It might even be best to wait for the captain, because before they can claim anything, they have to present a Bill of Lading."

Eli finished gearing up the animals and led them from the stables and onto the deck at the planks. The grey was on a long lead that was dallied around the saddle horn and followed close behind the big claybank stallion. Eli led the two down the plank, intentionally paying little attention to the stacked cargo and those beside it. The captain followed the horses down the plank, the chaplain with him, and they walked to the cargo, ostensibly to take inventory of the remaining goods. Eli turned to his horses, checking the gear, as he listened to the men confront the captain and the chaplain.

"Are you the captain?" asked Skip Martin, one other man standing slightly behind him but both looking to the men.

"That's right. What do you need?" asked Captain Marsh.

"There's some cargo that was supposed to be aboard the *Louella* that we don't see here. We were told it would be unloaded and made available."

The captain nodded to the considerable goods, boxes, and barrels, "The only cargo that is not stacked there are the cattle that are still on board. Just what were you expecting, and do you have a Bill of Lading for that?"

"Uh, we represent the Blackfoot Mission, and we were expecting several boxes of Bibles and books and other supplies, but we don't see them here," stated Martin, motioning to the stack of goods.

"Bill of Lading?" asked the captain.

"Uh, we don't have one right now, but we can get one. Those papers were given to the freight company that was supposed to pick up the cargo at Cow Island, but they did not return with the cargo, so we could only assume it was still aboard."

The captain glanced toward Eli, saw him approaching the group, and feigned attention to the cargo, frowning as if he expected to find the missing cargo buried among the stack of goods. Eli spoke from behind him, "Any trouble here, Captain?"

"You! You're still buttin' in where you don't belong! I've had enough of you!" growled Martin, pushing past the captain and chaplain. He was grabbing for his belt pistol as he glared at Eli, but Eli casually held his Colt before him and cocked the hammer. The racketing sound of the cocking hammer stopped Martin where he stood. He looked wide-eyed down at the pistol and up at Eli.

"Well, what was that you were going to do? Best get at it, because I'm gonna take you to the fort and turn you over to the commandant. And I have it on good authority, the commandant doesn't like gunrunners."

Martin let a slow grin split his face, "Hah!" he grunted, and forced a laugh. "Shows how much you know." He nodded toward the stockaded fort, "That ain't nuthin' but a trading post of the Northwest Fur Company, ain't been no sojers in there since the Blackfoot run off the last ones! Now, what'chu gonna do, mister high'n mighty?" growled Martin. He stood tall, tucked his thumbs behind his belt, and said, "Drop that there pistol and I'll take you down a notch or two for gettin' muh pards kilt!"

Eli glanced to the captain and back to Martin. He slowly holstered his pistol, unbuckled the pistol belt, watched as Martin dropped his pistol, and slipped off his jacket. Eli started to strip off his jacket, but Martin grinned, cackled, and cut loose a haymaker while Eli's hands were tangled in the sleeves of his jacket. Eli jerked his head to the side and took the glancing blow as he shed his coat.

Eli stepped into Skip, brought his fist from behind his knee and buried it into the gut of the outlaw. Skip was bent over, gasping for air as Eli clasped his hands together and brought down a hatchet blow to the back of Martin's head, driving his face into the sand. Martin sputtered and scrambled back to his feet, wiping the sand from his face and eyes just as a roundhouse blow caught him on his jaw. Eli heard the crunch of bone as the man's jaw was knocked askew.

Martin grabbed at his face as he staggered backward. But anger flared in his eyes as he flexed his fists and snarled and charged toward Eli. The outlaw growled and screamed as he charged, but Eli deftly stepped aside, burying his fist in the man's belly again. Martin rolled off Eli's fist and brought a looping left around to crash against the side of Eli's skull, driving him off his feet and falling to the ground. Martin roared and lifted his big hobnailed boots to stomp on Eli's head, but Eli rolled away, grabbing the uplifted leg of Martin, and pulling it up, lifting Martin off balance and causing him to fall onto his back, with a thud that took the man's breath.

Eli rolled away, jumped to his feet, and nimbly stepped toward the downed Martin, but Martin, gasping and snarling, grabbed at his pistol that lay on the ground beside him, glaring at his prey, and growling as he lifted the pistol, cocking it and readying to fire, but Eli snatched the Bowie knife from his back and with one motion, threw it to bury it in the man's chest, driving into the hilt of the long-bladed knife, Martin's bullet whipping by Eli's ear. Martin's eyes flared with fear and rage as he looked at the knife, started to speak, his fingers closing on the haft of the knife, but blood gurgled up in his mouth and anger flared in his eyes, as they went sightless, staring at the empty sky. His arms fell to his side, his fingers loosed on the knife and life slipped away.

Martin's partner growled as he grabbed his pistol, but the captain, who held Eli's holstered pistol, brought up the Colt and dropped the hammer before the man could fire. He turned his startled eyes to the captain, mumbled, "But, but..." and crumpled to the ground, blood and foam bubbling from his open mouth.

Eli looked at the captain, glanced to the chaplain, and said, "Thanks. I reckon that balances the books." He took his belt and holster from the captain, slipped the pistol in the holster, and said, "So, Chaplain, I guess that means you'll be going to Helena to start that church for the miners?"

The chaplain nodded, forced a smile, "It has been said that the Lord works in mysterious ways, His wonders to perform. So..." he shrugged.

"Then along those lines, I need to find the mysterious livery to put my horses up and meet with my fellow travelers to make plans for them to get to Helena."

"Oh, is Constance going to Helena?" asked the captain.

"No, her business is here, I think, but I need a favor..." began Eli. He continued to explain about his dinner date with Constance, and his plan to have supper with the Hamiltons and Williamses to help get them on their way to Helena. "So, if you'll take my place at dinner with Constance, I'll meet with the others."

The captain chuckled, "I'd be happy to, Eli. Any time I can have a fine dinner with a beautiful woman like her, I'm happy to oblige."

WITH HIS HORSES and gear put away at the livery, Eli went to the town marshal's office to give his story about Skip Martin and his crew of gunrunners. Since the captain and chaplain had already given their stories, the visit with the marshal was brief and pleasant. "Also, Marshal, I've been on the trail of my two stepsons, Jubal and Joshua Paine. They're twins and were last known to be working for Paquette's freighters. I did get word they might be going to the goldfields down by Helena, but nothing definite. Have you had any contact with them, or know anything about them?"

The potbellied grey-haired marshal leaned back in his chair and twisted the ends of his handlebar moustache, frowning at Eli as if he was thinking. "No, can't say as I have. The names aren't familiar to me and bein' twins, I reckon I'da recomembered runnin' into 'em. Would there be a wanted poster on 'em?"

"I don't think so, but I don't know everything that might have happened since they left the army. That was goin' on two years ago," offered Eli.

"Wal, in a couple years, young men can get into a peck o' trouble!" observed the marshal.

"You're right about that. They were raised by their mother, I was off to the army and war, but they come from good stock, so I've been hopeful. Well, Marshal, I'll check back with you the next time I'm in the area, for right now I'm bound to go south toward Helena and the goldfield to see..." he shrugged as he rose. After shaking hands with the less than enthusiastic or energetic marshal who kept his seat, Eli left the office.

With a quick stop at the bank to cash a bank draft, he went to the Rialto Hotel and secured himself a room. He picked up his bedroll and saddlebags from the floor beside the hotel clerk's counter, and with rifle in hand asked for the room number for the Hamiltons.

"That'd be number twenty-two. Upstairs, 'bout halfway down the hall, on the left. Your room, number twenty-six, is toward the end," stated the clerk.

"Thank you."

"And, we don't allow no shootin' in the hotel!" cautioned the clerk, trying his best to look stern and authoritative.

Eli stopped, looked at the clerk over his shoulder, and one-handed, flipped his rifle by the lever, bringing a bullet into the chamber and cocking the hammer, and with a frown to the clerk, "You don't *allow*? And just how do you do that?"

"Uh, uh...well, we *ask* our patrons to refrain from such activity."

"That's better. I will do my best to abide by your request," chuckled Eli, turning his back on the clerk and starting up the steps, carefully lowering the hammer on his rifle with his thumb and shaking his head with a wide grin on his face. This was not the first time he had dealt with greenhorns that thought they had authority to lord over others but did not have the spine to back up their bravado.

CHAPTER 34

SEPARATIONS

Eli stood beside the stagecoach, Harriet holding his hand between them, "How can we ever thank you, Eli?" she pleaded, "You've been an angel for us, in so many ways. Without you, I don't know what we would've done, and now..." she shrugged and tiptoed up to give him a hug. She looked up at him, "After we are reunited with Cyrus, you be sure to look us up because I know he will want to repay you."

"That's nothing to worry about, Harriet. It has been my privilege to know you and your family and to help in any way possible. If you need anything, just leave word with the local law and I'll find out, sometime," replied Eli. He looked to Luther and Mildred, "Luther, it is good to see you mending so well. Now, you and Ben," he glanced to the young man, "will be the only men for your two families and I'll be counting on you to see them safely home in Helena."

Luther chuckled as he reached out his hand to shake with Eli, "You've been a great friend, Eli, and if there's ever anything..."

"You just do your best to make a home for your family and see to Harriet and the youngsters getting home to Cyrus." He looked to Ben, "And that goes for you, too, Ben. I'm counting on the both of you."

"I won't let you down, Eli, and you be sure to come see us when you get down thataway," replied Ben, nodding to Eli but keeping his arm around Maribel's waist.

Eli stepped back as the two families boarded the stage; he noticed the name across the top of the stage above the doors had been recently painted over. Where before it had been *Overland Mail and Express*, it now read *Wells Fargo*. As everyone was seated, Eli saw there were two men, dressed like peddlers, that completed the nine passengers on the interior of the stage. He shut the door, stepped back and as the stage pulled out, he waved to the departing friends.

Eli walked into the mercantile, paused to take in the sight, sounds, and smells of the place, and recognized the odors of leather, gunpower, and more. With a broad smile he went to the counter, lay down his list of needs and looked at the clerk, "Reckon I need some supplies. They're all written down there if that'll help."

The clerk picked up the list, adjusted his glasses that hung on the end of his nose, looked it over, and glanced to Eli, "No mining supplies?"

"No, not doing any mining. But you might answer a couple questions for me."

"Shoot," offered the clerk as he sat the list on the counter, placed both hands on the counter and leaned toward Eli.

"I'm looking for a couple men, they're twins, young, might be headed to the goldfields. Do you recall seeing any twins come through, maybe buying some supplies?"

"Nope, can't say as I have." He looked from Eli to the list, "How you payin'?"

"Gold coin," answered Eli. "You have everything on the list?"

"I do. Let's see, cartridges, cornmeal, coffee...It'll take a bit to get it together."

"I'll wait," answered Eli, nodding to the clerk.

It did not take the man long to compile the goods, stacking them on the counter and writing things down. When he was finished and had tallied things up, he looked at Eli, "That'll be nineteen dollars an' fifty cent."

Eli grinned, reached into his pocket, and brought out a twenty-dollar gold piece, lay it on the counter and started packing his goods to the door and the packhorse tethered outside. In a short while, he stepped aboard his big stallion, reined him around to go to the Grand Hotel and bid his goodbye to Constance. They had lunch together, shared memories of their trip, and as they finished, Constance leaned forward and clasped Eli's hand, "I'm going to miss you, Eli."

"Oh, I might be back. It all depends..." he shrugged.

"I know, and I know that finding your sons is the most important because of the covenant you made with their mother. I respect you for that, but I do want to see you again," she added, still holding his hand, and smiling.

"You never know, Constance, by the time you finish your business, I might complete my task and we could meet one another again. But, if not, I know where you'll be in St. Louis, and I might have business there that could draw me back to the city, and if so, I'll be sure to look you up."

"I'd like that. But, please, be careful and try to keep in touch."

"I will," he said. He stood, helped her up and gave her a hug, pushed away, and held her by her shoulders, smiled, and said, "I want to remember you just like this."

Constance smiled, dabbed at her eyes with her hanky, wiping away tears, and smiled again. "Goodbye, Eli."

———

HE HAD NO SOONER PUT the crowds of the bustling town behind him when he took to the Mullan Road, headed south. He knew the road would take him to the goldfields, but before him in the far west rose the towering Rocky Mountains. And names like Alder Gulch, Virginia City, Hungry Hollow, Last Chance Gulch, and more would demand his attention as he continued on his quest to fulfill the covenant he made with his wife. It would require even more of a commitment than already given, for he knew he would be riding into a land filled with men that thought only of gold, riches to be had, and they had to get it before any others. That lust and greed often warped man's sense of right and wrong, and many would pay with their lives, never seeing an ounce nor the glitter of gold. He also knew that blood would mingle with the pristine waters that flowed from the mountains and carried the tiny flakes that make up the dreams of men, and that blood might well be from the very men he sought, his own stepsons.

Once free of the settlement of Fort Benton, he stood in his stirrups and breathed deep of the clear air, looking about at the flatlands of the wide plateaus, but the dust of previous travelers still lingered in the air, and the stench of smoke from the steamboats, campfires, and guns fouled the air that he had expected to be clear of any indication of man. He dropped into the seat of his saddle, slapped legs to the big stallion, "C'mon, Rusty, let's find some fresh air!" The big stallion seemed to understand and stretched out, his nose in the wind, his mane slapping at the face of his rider and his tail flying high. The little dapple grey matched the claybank stallion, stride for stride, and the trio of travelers put miles, sounds, and the stench of unwashed bodies behind them.

A LOOK AT BOOK TWO:
LAST CHANCE GULCH

It was a lawless land. A different time and different place than what most people had become used to when they lived in the eastern societies, but desperate men had come west seeking fortunes to build a new life. The civil war had destroyed homes, families, most everything they knew, and now, determined to build a new life, they came west in droves. The lure of riches in the gold field fueled their lust, their determination to succeed dimmed their morals, their commitment to become rich became the overbearing drive for everything they did or tried.

It was into this melee of madness that Eli McCain rode, committed to a search for his deserter sons to fulfill a covenant, a promise, to his recently departed wife. He came from years serving as an officer in the western forts and the front lines of the bloodiest war that man had known on the shores of the new land. But that was behind him, now he was bound for the gold fields of Montana territory, the new strikes in Last Chance Gulch that were said to be the richest yet and the possibility for riches had lured his sons west.

But this was a lawless land, sheriffs turned the other way, vigilantes rose up to bring some semblance of law and order, and into this rode a man whose life had always been committed to do right and to stand for right no matter the cause or cost. But he must put the search for his sons first, or could he? When the devil's crowd were painting the land with the blood of innocents, could he stand aside? Or would he take a stand?

AVAILABLE APRIL 2023

ABOUT THE AUTHOR

Born and raised in Colorado into a family of ranchers and cowboys, **B.N. Rundell** is the youngest of seven sons. Juggling bull riding, skiing, and high school, graduation was a launching pad for a hitch in the Army Paratroopers. After the army, he finished his college education in Springfield, MO, and together with his wife and growing family, entered the ministry as a Baptist preacher.

Together, B.N. and Dawn raised four girls that are now married and have made them proud grandparents. With many years as a successful pastor and educator, he retired from the ministry and followed in the footsteps of his entrepreneurial father and started a successful insurance agency, which is now in the hands of his trusted nephew. He has also been a successful audiobook narrator and has recorded many books for several award-winning authors. Now finally realizing his life-long dream, B.N. has turned his efforts to writing a variety of books, from children's picture books and young adult adventure books, to the historical fiction and western genres which are his first love.

CPSIA information can be obtained
at www.ICGtesting.com
Printed in the USA
BVHW040926170323
660662BV00016B/1832

9 781639 778102